Train journey
through the tides

A novel by

Chris Marfield

Book

Jack is on a train at the start of a journey. He is a simple man in his thirties, reliable, honest and a little grey. A young woman appears in the compartment and immediately fascinates the introverted Jack. For the young woman, he comes at just the right time to fill a void and heal a wound.

A shared journey begins, influenced by situations and encounters that uncover a dark, long forgotten secret and put their burgeoning trust to the test.

Author

Chris Marfield was born and grew up in Hannover, Germany in 1970. Now he lives and works in Berlin.

Chris Marfield

Train journey

through the tides

Bibliographic information of the German National Library:

The German National Library lists this publication in the German National Bibliography; detailed bibliographic data is available on the Internet at http://dnb.dnb.de.

1st edition

E-Mail: chris.marfield@gmail.com

Production and publisher: BoD - Books on Demand, Norderstedt

ISBN: 978-3-7578-8992-0

1

I'm wondering why I never have any recollection of the appearance of a woman I've met in the past and thought was pretty.

When I meet a less attractive woman, I remember her appearance, every single detail, for a long time. But the more attractive I remember her, the faster I forget what she looked like. I know that she had beautiful eyes, or a wonderfully firm body, or the way her hair lay. But the image becomes blurred and the details disappear ... too quickly.

It's different when I've been with a woman for a long time, looked into her eyes a thousand times or smelled her scent. Then it no longer matters whether she was pretty or not, because she was. That intimate bond that makes two people an unconditional unit. Then I remember her appearance down to the smallest detail and how the individual contours of her body felt.

It's like a part of me that's always been there and will always be there forever. Like a tattoo that smiles at me every time I look in the mirror.

Sometimes it's a really lovely memory that reminds me of a tender happiness. But this memory can also be painful, tearing a deep chasm, down into the dark soul, just like fate, which haunts us with things and deeds we never thought possible until we experienced them.

Jack looks up from his appointment diary and thinks about the lines he has just written on the blank note pages. These sentences came to him spontaneously, and without knowing why, he had an irresistible urge to write them down.

A big emotional outburst by his standards, something he rarely experiences. He sees himself as rational and sober, more of a civil servant type.

He thinks about the words of his ex-wife Brigitte, who described him as punctual, meticulous and grey. As grey as the simple cloth trousers he likes to wear with his plain coloured shirts. Jack puts the appointment diary back in the inside pocket of his jacket, which he has carefully hung on a hook.

The window of the compartment he is looking out of is brown with dust. But it doesn't affect the clarity with which he sees the people and their absurdities on the crowded platform. People are squeezing into the train, where Jack has long since secured a good seat thanks to his punctuality. He has already stowed his leather suitcase, with its shiny metal fittings, safely on the luggage rack.

The compartment smells musty, like a worn-out room where countless people, animals and pieces of luggage have spent their time travelling from one destination to the next.

The conductor stands at the edge of the platform with stoic composure. Unimpressed by the hustle and bustle around him, the screaming children, the quarrelling couples and the tears of farewell.

A man approaches completely rushed the train, carrying a heavy suitcase and two travelling bags. Exhausted, he loses his balance and falls lengthways onto the platform. The suitcase bonces open and spilling its contents, a few shirts, ties, trousers, socks and some underwear. Cursing, his head red, he stuffs his things back into the suitcase, which can no longer be closed. Something keeps peeping out, making it impossible to lock it properly. Finally, he takes the suitcase in his headlock and walks quickly to the carriage, where he jumps in with a sigh of relief.

A mother with a child in her arms rolls a trolley, beside her a man carrying two large bags.

Jack wonders whether it is her brother, a friend or perhaps her husband. The child is crying with a snivelling expression. Its face is streaming with tears and its nose is running. The woman says something to the man and makes a condescending gesture. Then she speaks to the child, as she has probably done countless times before. The words do not have the desired effect and the child's crying is now accompanied by a piercing scream. She says something to the man again, who nods uncertainly, and gets on the train with the child, who is still screaming. The man follows her and comes out a few moments later, standing on the platform in front of the compartment where the woman obviously still has something to say.

Inside the carriage, the rumble of stray passengers, which had been audible all the time, intensified. Most of the travellers have found their destination on the train and are now stowing their luggage, some of them making a crashing noise.

The platform thins out, there are fewer people and it gets quieter. A few stragglers, consisting of a group of young men and women, hurry up laughing and head for the door to jump in with a skillful bound.

Shortly afterwards, a whistle shrills through the air and the train starts to move with a jolt.

At first, Jack barely notices the departure, but then the station passes him by like a film until it disappears from his view. With a contented sigh, Jack leans back into the seat and enjoys the silence in the compartment. He watches a car that seems to be racing the train, but a traffic light lets the train win.

The cityscape dissolves, dense blocks of buildings give way to small detached houses, until greenery takes the place of concrete and tarmac. In the distance, hills rise, becoming more and more like mountains, their peaks still covered in snow and glistening in the sun despite the spring.

Jack sees his face reflected in the window. The short-cropped blond hair, the narrow, bony cheeks and the pointed chin. His face is as thin as his whole body. Although he is in his mid-thirties, he looks a good five years younger, thanks to his balanced lifestyle.

He strokes his fingers over his right cheek, where there is a scar the size of a thumbnail. He touches the smooth surface of the now healed wound with his fingertips, which reminds him again and again of the dark side of himself.

A time as a victim and a perpetrator that turned him into the person he never thought he was. But the past is real and is now a part of him that he will carry with him like a dark shadow for the rest of his life.

2

Slowly, and with a heavy squeak, the compartment door is pushed open. A young woman stands in front of it and opens it with some effort. She pushes her way into the compartment through the not quite open gap, carrying a large travelling bag in front of her. She uses her knee to manoeuvre the bag onto the middle seat and then sits down directly opposite Jack at the window.

Only now does she seem to notice Jack and greets him with a cool smile, accompanied by a barely perceptible nod.

He says a fleeting "hello" to her, looks at her briefly, but immediately turns his gaze away and looks out of the window. He sees her reflection in the window pane and looks at her curiously. The young woman also looks out of the window and their eyes meet, whereupon he reflexively averts his gaze. He looks off into the distance, as if there is something interesting to see that needs his attention right now. He can feel his own breathing, which is faster than usual as it tries to synchronise with his pounding heart.

A few minutes of silence pass, during which Jack avoids looking at her. But the urge is so strong that at first he catches a glimpse of her reflection out of the corner of his eye, and then, as if drawn by some strange force, he blinks at her, only to quickly avert his gaze again.

He can't estimate how long they've been sitting there, but now the silence is broken by a rustling sound caused by her hands rummaging in her travelling bag. She pulls out a walkman, a book and an apple. She carefully unwinds the headphone cable from the Walkman and puts on a pair of headphones. She switches on the walkman and opens the book, holding it in one hand and the bright green apple in the other. Satisfied, she takes a big bite of the apple and begins to read.

The soft melody of a violin fills the room with a hum. Jack leans back in his seat, listening to the gentle sounds of the music and daring to look at her timidly. She reads without taking her eyes off the book, her gaze fixed on the lines. He can see that the book is by Nietzsche, but he can't make out the title, which is covered by her fingers.

His gaze moves down her body to her legs, which she has casually crossed. She is wearing light-coloured jeans and a green t-shirt, through which the shape of her breasts can be seen. Jack catches himself wondering what her body might feel like, squinting at her legs, her breasts and her narrow shoulders. Her black hair is cut short, except for the fringes that fall boldly across her forehead. Her warm brown eyes work their way earnestly through the lines of the book.

He now looks unabashedly at her face, his gaze sweeping over her feminine features. She has a small mouth with thin lips and large eyes with thick brows. Her cheekbones are finely defined and there is a small birthmark on her narrow chin. He is particularly struck by her smooth skin, which looks pale in contrast to her dark hair. In a mysterious way, she seems gentle and sensitive to him.

The longer he looks at her, the more character traits he assigns to her. Her eyes ... loving, her mouth ... gentle, her breasts ... sexy, her hair ... self-confident. Bit by bit, she gets a profile, he takes away a little here, rounds off a little there. Like a sculptor, he moulds her so that she takes on more and more shape beyond her appearance. From Maria Magdalena to Jeanne d'Arc to the pop star Madonna. She is the best of all.

She takes a last bite and puts the half-eaten apple into a small bag, which she stows in her travelling bag, before continuing to read the book. Her leg is very close to his, almost touching. He feels a caress on his calf and looks down, but her leg is still a few centimetres away from his calf.

He shifts restlessly on the seat. He can feel drops of sweat making their way down his back under his shirt. He looks out at the landscape, at the fields passing by, but the distraction remains a futile attempt.

Her image is in front of him the whole time, wherever he looks.

He breathes in deeply and holds his breath. He remains like this for a few seconds until he slowly lets the air out again through his nose.

He looks at trees, the mountains in the background, a stream and... her reflection in the glass. This beautiful woman attracts his gaze like a magnet. He examines her upper body, imagines how her skin smells, then his eyes wander down her flat, almost muscular stomach. The short t-shirt reveals a few centimetres of skin, as taut as he imagines her whole body to be.

Sighing softly, he lays his head back against the cushion and looks at her face out of the corner of his eye. Then he closes his eyes, visualising her image in his mind. He dozes off with a mixture of shame and a rare feeling of happiness.

A click that silences the hum of the walkman brings Jack out of his thoughts. Relaxed, she looks out for a while and then turns her head towards him. She looks into Jack' eyes and shows the beginnings of a smile. He can't withstand her gaze and looks out of the window indecisively.

Then he decides to break the silence. He points to the book, the title of which he can now recognise. It is The Dawn.

"Interesting book," he says, pointing to the book.

"Really? It's not often you meet someone who likes books like that," she says with a smile.

"I like books like that. I particularly like Nietzsche."

"I really enjoy reading Nietzsche, he has something frightening, but also something comforting. In the end, however, I always feel like I'm going round in circles."

"Maybe that's exactly what he's trying to tell us."

"That we're going round in circles?"

"Yes, I like his thoughts on the will of the Force. We go round and round in circles, over and over again. I would even go a step further. It's like clockwork... all cogwheels... some big, some smaller. By the time one wheel has turned, others have already turned several times. But they all have one thing in common. They always turn in the same circle."

"That would mean that everything in life repeats itself," she says, frowning.

"It's not always the external things that repeat themselves. We ourselves also go through the same cycle again and again. Zarathustra beautifully describes how human beings change from camel to lion, and then from lion to child ..."

"I've read that," she interrupts him. "But I think it's a bit too easy to reduce people to that. I think there's a lot more going on with people. When I think back to my adolescence, I've already gone through a few more changes," she says, touching her forehead.

"Yes, just like a clock, where the gogwheels are turning, some more, some less. What you experience over many years also happens on a small scale. On a single day you wake up as a camel, during the day you become a lion and in the evening you retire peacefully as a child."

She looks at Jack long and thoughtfully, frowning and stroking a finger over her temple.

"It's possible, but I don't think that's what he wanted to tell us," she says and continues reading without paying any further attention to him.

Jack feels a heat rising inside him and has the feeling that he is blushing. He looks out of the window and wonders why he had to say such nonsense.

An oncoming train hisses past them. It gets dark for a moment and the carriage swings in the wind. He watches the carriages of the oncoming train pass like a storm of flashing lights, and as suddenly as the other train was there, it is gone.

What follows is a silence that seems even emptier and quieter than before, as if all sound had been sucked into a vacuum.

"Are you on a business trip?" she suddenly asks in the silence. Jack flinches, so surprised is he by the question. She looks at him with such disarming frankness that he is taken aback for a moment.

With a big step, she invades his territory. She speaks to him with such direct frankness, as if they were old friends... and he likes it. She looks at him so directly and purposefully that it gives him a feeling of familiarity. There must be a few years between them, and he could easily take this directness as disrespect, but he does not. He feels flattered and, even more than that, he feels comfortable. Even if it's just a question, he perceives this direct approach as a step into his personal intimate space, which people usually avoid when they don't know each other.

"Something like that," he replies, not knowing why he is acting so secretive.

Unimpressed by his answer, she continues. "I'm going home, I've finished my diploma."

"Congratulations," he says hesitantly. He is almost a little embarrassed by his curt reply, because finishing her degree is certainly a big deal for her. But he can't think of anything more appropriate. Then he adds: "What did you study?"

"Social sciences, I actually wanted to study psychology, but somehow I would be so limited. With this degree, I just have more opportunities in different areas. I mean, as a psychologist, I'm a psychologist and that's it. But what if I can't do that? Then I'll look pretty stupid."

He ponders her words for a moment. "What's wrong with being a psychologist?"

"Well," she stammers, "what if it gets too much for me to deal with everyone else's problems? Maybe I don't have the thick skin I need. What if I'm confronted with people who are broken and really need help? What if I'm not able to help them, or I can't cope with the problems of others myself?"

He looks at her understandingly. "Do you have a job lined up?"

"To be honest, no. I don't really have an idea what I should do yet," she says a little helplessly.

Feeling he has cornered her, he considers changing the subject.

Finally, he asks her where she comes from and what she does in her spare time. She talks openly about her family, her friends and her flatmates in the flat they share. She answers his questions openly and doesn't mind his growing curiosity.

She grew up in a sheltered home with two older brothers, but secretly always wanted a sister. School was no problem for her, she passed her A-levels easily.

At the age of fourteen, she climbed out of the window on Saturday nights to go to the disco with her friend, where they danced the night away. Her parents could never understand why she slept until noon on Sundays.

She also shares her first experiences of using drugs with him. She talks about how bad she felt after her first joint and how good it felt once she got used to it. Jack' eyes widen when she tells him that she still smokes marijuana from time to time. In her youth, she was often the centre of attention and many people wanted to be friends with her. But at the age of twenty-four, she has now shed the coolness she once had.

Just natural, a lovely person, he thinks as she speaks. Her eyes shine and her face lights up, awakening a feeling of affection in him. He watched the way she moved her lips, the gestures she made with her hands to embellish her stories and, above all, her facial expressions, which had something unique about them.

Now and then she also asks Jack questions, which he answers more and more openly. He even goes further and tells her more than she actually wants to know.

He then casually asks her about a boyfriend, but she evades the question, which only makes him more curious. But that is the end of the conversation for the moment.

In the distance, he can see a large mountain that they are heading straight for. He imagines how they would crash if there was no tunnel. But as soon as he finishes this thought, it gets dark. The light in the train does not switch on in time, so it is completely dark. She is silent, and he says nothing either, listening to the monotonous sound of the train as it glides heavily over the tracks and continues its relentless journey. He feels at ease in the dark backdrop that lies protectively over him, until the light abruptly switches on and spreads brightly.

"Would you mind looking after my things for a moment?" she breaks the silence as she stands up.

"Yes, of course," he replies, a little surprised, and looks after her as she briskly walks out.

3

Her travelling bag, carefree left behind, lies ajar next to her seat. Without approaching the bag, his curious gaze falls on it. He can only make out a little, and what he sees could be anything. Pleased by her trust and ashamed of his own curiosity, he averts his gaze and looks at the now empty seat opposite him.

Where she had just been sitting, it now looks dull and cold, just like the whole compartment, grey and pale. It's like a theatre backdrop that only gains colour with the right actors.

Jack takes the appointment diary out of his jacket and looks to see if there are any important appointments for the next few days. He doesn't find any important appointments. Actually, he never finds any appointments, it's just this typical automatic grasp that happens unconsciously over and over again.

Looking at the empty seat, he realises he doesn't even know her name yet. They had reached a depth in their conversation so quickly that there was no opportunity to introduce themselves.

There was such a sudden sense of intimacy that the obligatory opening phrases were washed over, as if by a huge wave, invisible at first, that suddenly came out of nowhere. No opportunity to decide to build an official bridge from the distance into the intimate realm.

His mind wanders back to the time he was introduced to his ex-wife. It was at a party and his friend Bernd introduced them to each other. Her name was Brigitte. With a knowing smile, she approached Jack with a matter-of-factness that amazed him. She had such an engaging manner that it seemed like fate to him. They were both alone at the party, had already heard of each other, and now they had met.

Everything seemed arranged, but he didn't mind, he even liked it. They met, and without a doubt they both knew that their separate paths would become a common one.

At the time, he had been through several relationships and had little hope for what he had only read about in books.

With her blonde braid, slim, expressive appearance and disarming smile, she enchanted him from the very beginning.

It took them two years to get married. Another two years before they divorced.

To this day, he finds it hard to understand how this relationship could fail. At that time, he never had any doubts about their bond. They cared for each other and read each other's wishes from their eyes. But caring killed the libido. Passion turned into friendship, friendship turned into indifference. Indifference led to nothing.

It was too perfect for love. That certain roughness that two surfaces need to rub against each other until they finally stick together was missing right from the start. They were like two sheets of ice sliding over each other and then separating without any brakes. And yet the end affected him deeply. He still remembers how irritated he was that it had shaken him so much. Even today, he feels an oppressive emptiness when he thinks of Brigitte. An emptiness that makes him angry because it still affects him. A period of depression and disorientation followed. Brigitte has since remarried. Now, four years later, Jack is still single.

Still looking at the empty seat, his thoughts return to the nameless woman who was sitting opposite him just a few moments ago. He thinks about how unreal the here and now seems to him. As if in a dream, he wonders how real it all is and if she exists at all, as he perceived her to be.

Der Drang, ihr nahe zu sein, wird mit jedem Moment ihrer Abwesenheit stärker. Er versucht, sich an ihr Gesicht zu erinnern, aber er kann es nicht. Er kann sich an alles erinnern, ihre Augen, ihren Mund... aber er kann das Bild in seinem Kopf nicht vervollständigen.

The door to the compartment opens and she is back as quickly as she had disappeared. She has freshened up her eau de toilette and a scent of lotus surrounds her. Gradually, the whole compartment is bathed in this flowery scent and the surroundings are transformed from pale grey to an exotic sea of colour.

"Thank you for looking after my things," she says, smiling familiarly at him.

"You're welcome."

They look into each other's eyes for a few seconds, a few moments longer than strangers would. There is a bond in that look, a pact that they make without words. It is not a promise, just an invisible bond that they forge and that fills Jack with happiness through and through. Her eyes shine at him and he feels that light warming him from within.

They sit in silence for a while, watching out of the window as the world passes by. The train passes through a wooded area. Trees cut through the warm sunlight and cast short shadows. Again and again a cool shadow flies over them for a split second. Each time it is like a brief stroke on the face. Then the train leaves the forest and the sun shines warmly on their faces.

4

She stands up, grabs her travelling bag and hefts it onto her lap as she falls back into her seat. Her legs form an X, her knees almost touching and her feet pointing inwards. She rummages in her bag and shortly afterwards reveals a paper bag with printed fruit symbols. She also takes out an empty plastic bag and then, without further attention, heaves the travelling bag back onto the seat next to her.

"Do you like cherries?" she asks, and without waiting for an answer, she sits down next to Jack and holds out the bag of cherries to him. She forms the empty bag into a box and places it on her thigh. Again charmed by her disarming directness, he watches as the first cherry disappears between her lips and she pulls off the stem with a plucking motion of her hand. He does the same and takes a cherry. The sour flavour spreads through his mouth, leaving a tingling sensation on his palate that makes him smile.

They sit so close together that their thighs are touching. He feels her warmth spread through his whole body via his leg. He picks up another cherry and bites into it, savouring the sour taste. He takes the cherry pit out of his mouth with two fingers and drops it into the box resting on her thigh. With a thud, the pit falls the last few centimetres down to the rest of the cherry pits. Now she lifts the box slightly and spits a pit into it in a high arc, followed by an amused giggle.

"What do you do?" she asks casually, then spits out another pit.

"I work in accounting for a wholesale company."

"OK, what are you doing there?"

"I'm responsible for monitoring financial transactions and invoices."

"And what exactly are you monitoring?"

"Well, when I receive an invoice, I check whether the total is correct and that the order number matches the purchase order. I also check whether the invoice is signed and if the date is correct. Finally, I check the cost centre."

"So you have to get a huge pile of invoices every morning, spend the whole day checking that everything is correct and then hand them in for payment?"

"Well, it's not quite that simple," he replies with a jovial smile.

"And what's it like then?" She spits the next cherry pit into the bag in a high arc.

"First an invoice comes in, resulting from an order process. Then the invoice goes to the person who ordered it, who is the first to check and sign it."

"I see, then you get the bill, check it and hand it over for payment."

"Not quite. The orderer has to get the invoice signed by his manager, who also has to check the content. After all, he is the one in charge."

"Oh, I see." She raises her eyebrows and looks at him in disbelief.

"But then I really get the invoice, check it and pass it on."

"You pass it on? Doesn't the company want to pay at some point?" she asks with a laugh.

"My boss does a final plausibility check. This involves checking whether there really is an order for the invoice and if the order details match those on the invoice."

"And the business is making money?"

"Yes, the company is quite profitable, we're even expanding."

"And how do you make money? Let me guess, you deal in paper," she bursts out laughing.

"We deal in electronics for the household sector. Coffee machines, kettles, toasters, etc."

"Oh, then I can buy a coffee machine from you."

"Unfortunately, that's not possible. We don't sell these items to private households."

"Who do you sell them to?"

"To the retail trade. That's where you can buy your coffee machine."

"You're a complicated business."

"Standards are important to us. They help us to be efficient and allow us to focus on our core processes, which in turn is a success factor for our business."

"And do you enjoy your job?"

"I admit there are more exciting things. But I'm well paid and I have security."

"I see," she says thoughtfully, looking out and watching a tractor ploughing. Blooming fields are lined up one after the other, symmetrically arranged, stretching far across the land until they are broken by the cloudless sky on the horizon.

"Do you have a girlfriend?" she asks with a cheeky grin out of the corner of her eye.

"No, I'm divorced," he says, wondering why the question touches him so much. It's been so long and yet it hits him like a blow. It's not even the thought of Brigitte, it's the question itself that digs deep into his heart and gives him a sinking feeling.

"How long have you been divorced?"

"Four years."

"And no new wife?"

"No, it took me a while to come to terms with it all. Once I had come to terms with it, I somehow forgot to think about a new relationship. Maybe I didn't want it, maybe it just didn't materialise."

"Don't you get lonely sometimes?"

"The first time after the divorce I was quite lonely. Later I thought about it less and less. I no longer knew what was actually hurting me. Was it the longing for my ex-wife or the loneliness? Maybe it's the longing for the fateful things that might lie ahead of me. It's what I don't know if it exists or, if it does, whether I will find it on my way."

"What do you miss most about your ex-wife?"

"There isn't one particular thing or quality that I miss the most. It's more the things we experienced together that I know are irretrievably gone. I know that I can't repeat these things with anyone else, at least not in this form and with the feeling that goes with it."

"But you can do things with other people that you might not have been able to do with her. You might even like those things a lot more."

"That would be nice," says Jack, noticing a bright spot on the opposite wall. He hadn't noticed it before. He hasn't really noticed his surroundings since this woman appeared in the compartment.

"Strange," he says in a thoughtful tone. He looks her straight in the eye. It's the first time he's looked at her with such intimate intensity.

"What is it?" she asks, gazing back at him curiously. They sit like this for a few seconds, looking into each other's eyes. Jack savours this moment of intimacy, which he would never have allowed himself with a strange woman. But here it's different. She has invaded his space and is sitting there with a white flag that he has also hoisted and is delaying and savouring this moment.

"I don't even know your name yet. I completely neglected to ask you."

"I could have told you," she replies understandingly.

She takes the bag of cherries and places it carefully on the table. She puts the box next to it, which is now overflowing with cherry pits. With a playful grin, she collapses into the seat and leans close to Jack.

"What about you, do you have a boyfriend?"

"I've been single for exactly three weeks," she says with exaggerated joie de vivre.

"What happened?"

"I caught him with someone else."

"That must be awful for you."

"It was just awful at first. I was so angry that I had no energy left for other feelings. Now I've closed that chapter and hardly think about it."

"You must be fed up with the world of men."

"No, not really. It's not the other guy's fault that he's such a jerk."

Her voice has softened and her eyes have lowered. Jack puts his hand gently on her forearm, whereupon she tilts her head slightly to one side. At this moment, it's obvious that she has the images of the past before her eyes and that she is suffering from them. Thoughtfully, but without a tear, they remain like this for a while.

Loud voices from a lively conversation can be heard from the neighbouring compartment. Laughter from several people, then silence, leaving only the steady sound of the train.

"My name is Abelia," she suddenly says into the silence.

"What does the name mean?"

"It's derived from Abel."

"Do you know why your parents gave you this name?"

"They never told me exactly. Maybe it was just a warning to my brothers, I don't know," she says with an ironic grin.

"I think it's a very nice name."

"Ever since I found out the name is connected to Abel, I've hated it."

"Maybe your parents had something completely different in mind when they gave you that name. Maybe they named you after the plant."

"What kind of plant?"

"It is a plant from the south with beautiful rose-coloured blossoms. It is said to be wonderfully fragrant and always in bloom. But it's too sensitive for our latitudes, it doesn't tolerate frost."

"Named after a flower, I like that much better," she says, smiling softly to herself.

"What does your name mean?" she asks after a while.

"Just Jack. Actually my name is Jack-Joachim. A name I'm not really proud of."

"Why is that? It's a nice name, isn't it?"

"It's a name for older people. My grandfather was called Jack. Nobody wants to be called that anymore."

"Your parents must have meant well. I'm sure they thought you'd be a Jack of all trades."

"Or a Jack of no trades," he replies laconically, making Abelia laugh out loud. She reflexively puts her hand to her mouth and pinches his side, then leans back against him.

5

With a jerk, the compartment door bursts open. A middle-aged man stands legs apart in front of them. Jack looks up at the man, who casts a dark shadow in the compartment. The man's size is easy for Jack to judge ... huge, towering over him by a good head's length. He wears his blond hair down to his shoulders and the rest of him invites Jack to hate him too, his figure is extremely athletic.

He is wearing tight trekking trousers with large side pockets and an even tighter white shirt, the short sleeves threatening to rip from his pumped-up biceps. The shirt is wide open, revealing the base of his pectoral muscles. A medallion dangles from a thick chain around his neck.

The man smiles at both of them, looking first at Jack, then at Abelia, before finally turning to Jack.

"Do you have a seat left for me?" he asks, and before Jack can answer, the stranger looks at Abelia. Wordlessly, she points to the seat by the door, diagonally opposite her.

He heaves his large rucksack onto the luggage rack with a flourish, as if it were filled with cotton wool. He drops into the seat with his legs apart and looks at them both with a friendly smile. They both avoid his gaze, resulting in an oppressive silence.

"I'm Rob," the stranger says unimpressed, still smiling.

"Abelia."

"Jack."

"I'm really glad there's room in your compartment. All the other compartments are full. It wouldn't be a problem now, as I have to get off at the next station anyway. But I really can't stand it any more at the moment. I've been climbing for the last few days and everything hurts at the moment."

"I'm sure your muscles are pretty sore," says Jack with an undercurrent of malicious glee.

"Have you been mountain climbing all by yourself?" asks Abelia, not waiting for an answer to Jack's comment.

"I usually go mountaineering alone. Of course, you can go with a group, but that's not really for me. Let's be real, together you only hinder each other. One person wants to climb fast, the other thinks it is too fast. I'm usually the faster one and then I have to wait all the time."

Rob starts talking about how he recently conquered a mountain massif in Nepal. He talks very animatedly, making big sweeping gestures with his hands.

After a while he stops paying attention to Jack and looks only at Abelia. She follows him attentively, nodding politely and occasionally asking a short question, which he answers with exaggerated seriousness. He answers her questions very carefully, explaining everything and looking intensely into her eyes.

Jack watches the two of them talk. Rob has turned to face Abelia, attentive but a little pushy, he thinks. She is sitting neutrally in her seat, her legs casually crossed, her toes pointing towards the stranger.

Motivated by the questions, he speaks at length, with opulent visual descriptions. His voice is deep and melodious. The vowels in some words are so melodiously drawn out that they seem to contradict his rugged appearance.

A large scar adorns his forearm. A thick vein protrudes from his bicep, stretching his shirt to the limit, as if trying to escape the oppressive mass of muscle.

The subject of mountaineering seems to have come to an end. Abelia has nothing more to ask and Rob seems to have nothing more to say. Satisfied, Jack notices that the stranger is running out of steam and can't help but feel a gleeful satisfaction. But as soon as he has finished his thought, Rob moves on, digging up the next adventure story. Abelia continues to listen attentively. She nods here and there, asks a question there and then, and sometimes a smile crosses her face.

Jack now feels completely excluded and humiliated as he sits unnoticed in his seat. He reflects on the fact that he is actually alone on this journey and that he has only spoken to her. No promises have been made and no hope has been raised. No, he alone is responsible for this, for the illusions of the saint that he has interpreted into her, and for the togetherness that he has felt.

Although he was there first ... and anyway ... this Rob can't know that they don't really belong together. They sit here together, side by side, chatting, touching, intimate in a way that strangers can't be. The guy bursts into this harmony and tries to hammer his way in between them. Jack is beside himself at the thought, his mouth starts to tremble, adrenaline shoots through his body.

Looking off into the distance, he takes a deep breath and blows slowly against the pane, which fogged up under his breath. He breathes in and out a few times, feeling his head pounding and his heart racing. The mist on the window dissipates, only to increase again with the next exhalation. The bigger the mist, the slower his heart beats. Gradually the anger subsides. The pounding in his head eases and he begins to breathe deeply and evenly. His head leans back against the seat, his shoulders slump as if of their own accord, and the beginnings of a grin form the corners of his mouth.

The train has slowed down, the fields passing them slowly until they pass through the centre of a village. Small half-timbered houses line the neatly cobbled streets. Flowers on windowsills and manicured front gardens are inviting. The village streets are narrow. Two cars are approaching each other, one stops in a traffic bay and lets the other pass. A man and a boy are squatting in front of a garage, pumping up the tyres of a bicycle.

They are passing a church. Tall and dark, it towers over everything around it. Even the biggest houses in the village look tiny next to it. The church rises up in front of the train so that Jack can no longer see anything but the big dark walls. Rob is now reflected in the dark window as he talks to Abelia. His blond head appears ghostly in front of these walls until they finally pass, the church disappears behind them, and half-timbered houses appear again, followed by a few farms, until the village landscape alternates with wide fields.

As Jack looks out at the landscape, he feels a cold and dull sensation in his chest. He feels as if he is surrounded by a great cold, which permeates him like ice, but prevents him from freezing because the cold itself insulates him.

He looks steeply down at the ground. Grass, rubble and stones rush past. It is impossible for him to recognise anything in detail. He tries to make out a single blade of grass... or a stone... or something. But it's impossible, everything rushes past him, no chance to catch anything in detail with his own eyes.

"What was your name again? Ayana?" Rob asks, obviously unable to remember her name.

"Abelia," she answers patiently.

"That's an unusual name, what does it mean?"

"It's a flower," she says gently, looking conspiratorially at Jack, who smiles at her in agreement.

Jack turns back to the two of them, relieved to have been brought back into the circle by her. How one word can create such a conspiratorial bond, he thinks, feeling almost a little superior to the intruder.

"Where does the name come from?" asks Rob, stroking his chin with his fingers. "It sounds Spanish or South American."

"That's right, the name is Spanish."

"So you're Spanish?"

"Half, my father is Spanish."

"I used to climb there too," says Rob, gazing wistfully into the distance.

"And where in Spain?" asks Abelia after a few seconds of silence.

Obviously expecting this question, Rob turns back to her to talk about his tour in north-east Spain. He spent some time in the Riglos Los Mallos area, where he has climbed various walls.

The train slows down and the houses of a small town line up one after the other. The closer they get to the centre, the more crowded the streets become. People fill the pavements, cars jam up at the crossroads.

A tinny announcement sounds over the loudspeakers and announces the next station, whereupon Rob looks up.

"I have to get off here." He grabs his backpack and pulls it out of the luggage rack with a deft movement. The backpack drops to the floor with a thud, slumps a little and then grinds to a standstill.

Then Rob sits down on the edge of the seat and leans over to Abelia. He touches her thighs with his hands and caresses them slowly, as if they have known each other for a long time.

"It was really nice to meet you. I haven't had such a good time in a while now," his lips sound melodious.

Abelia looks at him without saying anything. Jack's breath catches as he watches his hands move down her thighs. Images flash through his mind, too many images. He sits wordlessly, watching the scene.

Finally Rob stands up, taking his backpack and heaving it casually onto his back.

"Ciao, you two," he says as he leaves the compartment and takes another quick look back. He pauses for a moment before finally turning away and leaving the train.

6

They sit next to each other in silence for a while, each lost in their own thoughts.

As the train starts to move, Jack looks out onto the platform to see if Rob is still there, not sure if he wants to see him. But he is no longer there. He notices two clocks showing different times. On one clock, the second hand is trembling in place. It keeps moving on the twelve, wants to skip the number and then falls back again. The train picks up speed and they leave the station, pass through a residential area and leave the town, whereupon fields and woods reclaim the scenery.

"What do you think of Rob?" asks Abelia, her eyes fixed on the seat where he sat a few minutes ago.

"Kind of a weird guy. I don't think he has many friends."

"Oh, I don't think so. I think he has lots of friends."

"Maybe you're right. But he's definitely not going to be my friend." Jack waves it off as if he doesn't want to talk about it anymore.

"I think he's quite nice."

"Womankind will be at his feet."

"It's possible."

"Do you like him?"

"I don't know ... I don't think so ... I just think he's nice."

"Just nice?"

"I don't think he's good for love. He doesn't have enough to give to others."

"At least he has a lot to say," says Jack with a contemptuous grin.

"Yes, but not very varied."

"Isn't it always the same for all of us?"

"I'm sure you've got some things to talk about that are a lot more interesting than mountain climbing."

"And what do you have in mind?"

Abelia doesn't answer immediately. She looks at him with a deeply enquiring gaze.

After a few seconds, she says, "Tell me a secret."

"You think I have secrets?"

"Everyone has secrets."

"I only have a few secrets, and they'd better stay where they are."

"Why?"

"There are things that can change a whole life."

"Change is not a bad thing."

"Some are," he says seriously, his voice deep with the words.

"Now I'm curious, have you committed a crime?"

"And if I had?"

"It's your secret, and if you tell me, it will remain your secret. Only you will share it with me from then on."

Jack smiles, almost touched by this naive logic. He wonders if she is ready to shoulder this heavy burden with him.

"What if it's something bad?" he asks, looking deep into her eyes.

"Then it's okay," she says in a whisper.

"I killed someone," he says, looking down at his hands, folded in front of him.

"What happened?" she asks unperturbed.

Jack sighs, looks into Abelia's eyes for a moment, averts his gaze again and finally begins to tell the story. "He was a dog breeder from our neighbourhood. I never knew his first name, everyone just called him Göring. He kept the dogs in quite horrible conditions. Nobody ever noticed how he mistreated them. He used to walk them around the village. They were drugged, so nobody noticed how sick they actually were."

"How did you know they were sick?"

"It wasn't hard to recognise if you looked properly and wanted to see. Their bodies looked emaciated. You could see the pure misery in their eyes."

"How did you find out that he was abusing the dogs?"

"At some point I noticed a dog that was limping. I could see how much this dog was suffering. I followed Göring and watched him. When he was out of the village and felt unobserved, he walked faster. Too fast for the dog, who couldn't keep up. He just kept going, pulling hard on the lead that was wrapped tightly around his neck. The dog couldn't keep up, couldn't stay on his feet and fell. Göring moved on, dragging the dog behind him. I had never heard such a howl. I continued to follow him, and then I saw him kill the dog."

"What, just like that?"

"Just like that. He took a metal stake and hit the dog on the head three times. I suppose he was dead after the first hit."

"What happened after that?"

"He buried the dog in the woods near his house. I really blamed myself. I could have done something, but I just ran after him and watched."

Abelia says nothing, just listens. She looks at Jack attentively and encourages him with a nod to continue.

"From then on I watched him. From a hiding place in the woods, I watched the house with field glasses. I quickly realised what was going on. He was torturing all his dogs. He was kicking them, throwing all sorts of things at them, it was all extremely brutal. He had a van with a lot of cages in it. Sometimes he put some of the dogs in the van and drove off with them. He always came back alone."

"Did the man live alone? Didn't he have a family?"

"He didn't have a family, he lived alone with the dogs. One day I reported him to the police. The report was anonymous."

"Why anonymous?"

"Well ... you know ..."

"It's okay, I didn't mean to interrupt you ... sorry ... go on."

"I kept watching the house. At some point the police turned up at his house. They went into the house and obviously asked him some questions. He went with the police to the shed where most of the dogs were kept. They had a look around and then left."

"I'm sure they haven't found anything that makes him a criminal. Dogs aren't children, they don't look too closely when they're neglected or even mistreated," she mumbles to herself, lost in thought.

"One day he caught me."

She looks at him with wide eyes. "What happened?"

"I went to his house in the evening. It was dark and I could see him sitting in front of the television with a beer. I'd observed him so many times that I was sure he wouldn't move away ... He never did otherwise. So I went to the shed, which was never locked. The dogs were locked in cages, it was dark and quiet. Suddenly I felt a grip around my neck from behind. He was right behind me, I didn't even hear him coming. He was pushing me against one of the cages, the bars pressed into my face. I remember that I didn't feel anything, I was just shocked. Then he took an iron bar and hit the cage with it. The dog inside was so scared that it jumped up and bit my face. I didn't really notice it, there was just a feeling like a dull pressure. The dog bit a chunk out of my cheek."

Jack points to the scar on his right cheek with his finger.

"So that's where you got the scar." Abelia touches his scar with her fingertips. Her reaction is neither compassionate nor dismissive. She reacts as if she understands, as if pieces of a puzzle are gradually falling into place.

"He let go of me and I felt sick. I tried to get out, but he wasn't finished with me yet. He dragged me outside where he kicked me. Not in the face, just on my body. Then he told me to get lost and never show my face again, and that if I said anything to anyone, I'd get to know him properly."

"How did your family react?"

"I didn't tell them anything. I told my parents that some dog had bitten me, nothing more. I went to the doctor, who gave me a tetanus shot."

"Why didn't you report it?"

"I was sure that reporting him wouldn't have done much good. After all, I was the one who broke into his house. I decided to let some time pass, so I waited exactly six months. I counted every day until, six months later to the day, I went back to him and shot him."

"Just like that?"

"Just like that," says Jack in a firm voice.

He calmly tells her how he went to the house that evening and watched Göring through the window. As so often, he was sitting in front of the television, drinking beer. The sight of Göring frightened him, but his hatred was stronger. He broke a window pane with a stone and Göring came out. He had a baseball bat in his hand, which he swung threateningly. Jack walked up to him and, without a word, put the gun on him. Göring recognised him immediately, which made him even more afraid and caused his hands to tremble. It was difficult for him to hold the gun steady. Göring's eyes sparkled with such hatred and self-confidence that Jack knew there was no turning back. With trembling hands he pulled the trigger and there was a loud bang, followed by the thud of the lifeless body hitting the ground.

Then he ran to the shed and released the dogs. After that he ran home as fast as he could.

Jack takes a deep breath and looks at Abelia, whose eyes are focused on him. He can't look her in the eye right now, but he senses that she understands him. She has a hand on his shoulder, as if to protect him. A few moments of silence pass, then she asks: "Didn't the police find out? It's not easy to disappear in a small village like this."

"The police questioned some people in the neighbourhood who had been conspicuous in the past. They didn't come up with me."

"What happened to the gun?"

"The gun wasn't registered, I later sold it to an Albanian who took it back to his country."

"Where did you get the gun?"

"There was a group of marksmen in a neighbouring village who were known to have a good collection of weapons. I knew some of the guns had been bought off the books. I stole the gun from them."

"Didn't they keep the guns under lock and key?"

"They were very relaxed about it. They probably couldn't imagine that anyone would dare to steal from them. They were never sober at the weekends. I went there one Saturday night and took the gun. Of course, they didn't report it, and when the newspapers reported the murder, they must have been pretty nervous. They must have suspected that it was done with their stolen gun."

They sit side by side, staring at the wall in front of them. The sun is shining brightly, so brightly that they can see the dust dancing through the air like a dry mist.

"Did you regret it?" Abelia asks after a while, without taking her eyes off the wall.

"Sometimes," Jack says in a pressed voice after a long breath.

He thinks about the "sometimes" and how it affects him. He cannot grasp this »sometimes.« It is more a coming and going, depending on how it wants this »sometimes« to be or what kind of mood it is in.

He can never judge what mood the »sometimes«
will be in, or when it will return. It can be quiet for
months and he doesn't think about it at all. Or it might
come back after a few hours. But he can never predict
it. Like at this moment, it comes over him like a fever.
He feels hot and his pulse is so strong that he thinks
his neck will burst under the pressure of the blood being forced through the artery. The heat rises, his
hands tremble and sweat.

Abelia notices his trembling, damp hands on his
thigh. She takes one hand and places hers in it.

Only slowly does his hand stop trembling, it takes
minutes or hours. Her hand becomes damp and warm
beneath his. They melt together like precious metals
fusing at thousands of degrees to form an inseparable
alloy.

She leans close with her head, so close that he can
feel her breath on his skin. They watch in silence as
their hands play with each other, like a self-staged
play. She takes his hand with both of hers and holds
it tight. They sit like this for a while, feeling each other's warmth, without looking up or saying anything,
just listening to the monotonous sounds of the train.

7

A rumble comes from the corridor. Powerful footsteps stride through the carriage until the door of the neighbouring compartment is ripped open with a rolling grind.

"Tiiiickets, please," echoes to Jack and Abelia, who are still sitting there, lost in thought. The sound of the conductor's tongs being used to validate the tickets can be heard. A little later, the conductor is standing in front of their compartment. He scrutinises them for a moment and then pushes the door open.

"Tickets, please," he repeats his mantra, looking down at them with a combination of courtesy and equanimity. He seems to be photographing them with his eyes, comparing them in a fraction of a second with countless images in his head that he has already encountered that day. Abelia takes her ticket from the side pocket of her travelling bag, Jack takes it from the inside pocket of his jacket. The conductor takes the tickets one by one and, after a trained look at them, punches out the markings.

A man comes down the corridor and taps the conductor on the shoulder. "Excuse me, could you ..."

"Juuust a moooment," replies the conductor in a deep voice that seems to have been tuned down an octave for the words. He turns his head and looks sternly down at the man from the side. The man looks up intimidated and blushes, then takes a step back.

"One thing at a time. When I'm done here, I'll be pleased to help you," the conductor says in a stern tone.

The man lowers his head and takes a few steps away. Then he stops and makes an effort to come back. But a serious glance from the conductor makes him turn round again. He retreats and waits at a distance.

Now the conductor turns back to Jack and Abelia, who act as if they haven't noticed the scene.

"Everything has to be in order," he says. "I can't do everything at the same time."

He hands them their tickets back. "Are you travelling together?"

"In a way, yes," says Jack.

The conductor looks thoughtful and ponders for a long time. He pays no attention to the fact that someone is standing a few metres behind him with a request, then shakes his head almost imperceptibly.

"You know, I see hundreds of people every day. I come into contact with many of them and have a chat with some of them. I can see from a thousand metres away whether a couple is married or divorced, whether they have just argued or laughed together. I can even determine if the alleged father is really the father. It's just that I can't tell with you two. You look like you're belong together and yet actually you're not. You could be travelling together, but maybe you barely know each other, which I can't imagine."

Abelia laughs at him with amusement. "Maybe you're a little bit right about everything."

"That would explain it, but I don't want to be that indiscreet," he says a little more quietly in a conspiratorial tone. "But you must allow me one question."

They look at him and Abelia says: "Ask."

"Do you belong together or not?"

She looks at Jack, their eyes meeting with a certainty that knows no questions.

"Yes," she answers and after a pause: "We belong together."

"Well then, have a good journey," the conductor says with satisfaction, closes the door and continues on his way.

He has obviously forgotten the man who is still waiting in the corridor. The man turns back and forth a few times, then turns around and walks away.

"What you told me ..." says Abelia, without finishing the sentence.

"Yes?"

"No matter what you do to me ... I'll never tell anyone."

She sinks far back into the seat and leans her head against his shoulder. They sit there in silence without saying another word. Jack takes his arm and puts it around her so she can lean against him better. Then she closes her eyes. Her breathing becomes steadier and steadier until she finally begins to breathe automatically, like she does when she sleeps, as if she is being external controlled.

They now pass an industrial park, which is some distance away but still clearly visible. They can see a factory with huge halls and wide concrete walkways. Large chimneys made of red bricks rise up impressively like watchtowers. The smoke clears late in the sky, where it slowly spreads and dissipates in the loose clouds.

A warehouse with large white walls and countless roller shutters can be seen. There doesn't seem to be any work going on there, the hall looks unused and there are no people to be seen. At the edge of the industrial park, there are large car parks lined with cars and trucks, their windscreens reflecting the sun.

Jack leans his head against the window and watches as the industrial park moves further and further away, gradually becoming smaller and smaller until it disappears from view.

He feels the tiredness spreading through him and enjoys it. It is not the annoying tiredness he feels in the morning or often during the day. It is this pleasant heaviness, which is fine, because it is just right for this time, in this place, like after a long, hard day. He lets himself sink back into the seat and, thinking of this pleasantly heavy feeling, he falls asleep.

He sees himself in a large park. The midday sun is high in the sky, and the trees cast short shadows. Some people are out for a walk, others are having a picnic. Children are playing in a playground, parents are sitting on benches chatting. In the centre of the park is a large, elongated lake that cuts through the meadow like a wide river. On the other bank, he discover Abelia standing on a footbridge in a white dress. She waves to him, then goes to a rowing boat, sits in it and rows in his direction.

Suddenly he hears screams. A pack of dogs is running through the park, attacking the people. They jump up on the people and bite them savagely. Their fur is dark and dirty, their teeth look oversized, their eyes are blood red. People run screaming in all directions, some fleeing up a tree.

Jack looks at Abelia, who continues to row calmly in his direction, and laughs. He tries to stop her, shouting at her to stay put, but she just laughs. When she reaches the shore, she gets out of the boat and comes towards him. A dog crosses her path and stops in front of her, growling. She bends down and strokes the dog's head, whereupon it turns into a puppy. More dogs run towards her and she repeats the process with each one. Every beast she touches turns into a puppy.

Soon all the dogs have transformed under her touch and are jumping happily around the park. The humans come back, look around cautiously, then flock back to the meadows. Abelia comes up to Jack laughing, reaches out her hand and touches him on the shoulder.

He wakes with a wince, opens his eyes and sees trees passing by. The clouds have thickened and the sun is only visible pale behind them.

His first thought is of Abelia, still walking in front of him like a fairytale figure, as if in a dream. He looks ahead and sees her sitting in the square opposite again.

She has in-ear headphones in her ears and is listening to music. The synthetic sound of a violin fills the room. He recognises the melody, it's a ballet suite by Tchaikovsky. She doesn't notice that he's woken up and is looking at her. She has leaned back in a relaxed position with her right leg bent on the seat. She has placed her foot under the knee of the other leg. Her hands are relaxed on her bent thigh and holding an MP3 player.

Her gaze goes off into the horizon. She seems to be looking at something in the distance, sitting completely motionless. Perhaps she is not looking at anything at all, just staring aimlessly into nowhere.

They are crossing a valley with a small housing estate. Smoke rises from the chimneys of some of the houses, which are surrounded by meadows and trees. At the edge of the settlement is a lake where swans swim. The plumage of the adult swans is bright white, closely followed by the young, which look like grey balls of wool.

The music stops and he looks at Abelia, whose eyes are now fixed on him.

"I listen to music all the time, at every opportunity, and when I'm alone, I always have music on," she says thoughtfully.

"You like classical music?"

"Yes, I especially like classical music. But I also like jazz, latin and classic rock music. But mostly I listen to classical music."

"I also like listening to classical music, I like artists from the baroque period in particular. Bach is my favourite."

"I thought so," she says with a smile.

"Why?"

"Bach suits you. I bet you like his organ and piano pieces best."

"You're right, I do like them. How do you know that?"

"The pieces often sound like mathematical equations, as if they come from formulas that sound like rituals." After a short while she adds with a grin: "Just like you."

8

"Do you dance?" asks Abelia, looking at Jack inquiringly.

"Yes, I went through the standard dance course until I got my gold badge. Then I got into Tango Argentino and haven't danced anything else since."

"That surprises me. You don't really appear to be a tango dancer."

"I probably look too northern European for that."

"I mean more because the tango is so chaotic."

"Why do you think the tango is chaotic?"

"Well, no step is predictable, pure improvisation, anything goes."

"Improvising and possibly changing every single step only works if it follows certain rules. Otherwise you'd be stepping on each other's toes."

"Dancing on a rope with a net underneath."

"Yes, something like that," he says thoughtfully, whereupon images of the nightly dance events he used to regularly attend appear before him.

Lost in thought, Jack talks about the dance events, the milongas, that he loved. They never started before ten o'clock at night. He enjoyed this milieu, which always had a sinful atmosphere. The ambience permeated the dance hall like a melancholy fog. All the abysses found their place there and expressed themselves in a wordless passion.

He preferred to be alone at the milongas. Of course, he also regularly went dancing with Brigitte. But the magic of the tango had eluded them as a couple. There were no abysses, no melancholy and no noir for either of them. So there was no passion for them either. He only found the true tango when he was there alone.

"I like the tango," Abelia says, pulling him back from his thoughts. "But I only danced the tango a few times at dance school. Unfortunately, I didn't get beyond a few ochos and turns."

"You can do a lot with it. I could spend an evening dancing ochos and turns," Jack replies.

"It is said that you don't need much space to dance the tango. On the dance nights, the couples dance in the smallest of spaces."

"That's right, a telephone box would be enough for me," he says confidently.

"Then you could dance with me here?"

"Sure, it just needs music."

"I don't have any tango music."

"Then why don't you show me what you have?"

She gives him the MP3 player, whereupon he looks through the playlist and discovers some old rock songs that seem suitable. He marks Led Zeppelin with "Stairway to Heaven" and gives her the MP3 player back.

"What song?"

"I've marked it, you can start."

Abelia gets up and stands expectantly in front of him. She has the MP3 player tied to the side of her trousers with a loop. She takes one earbud from the headphones and puts it in her ear. He stands in front of her and lets her put the other earbud in his ear. She switches on the music and the first gentle chords of an acoustic guitar can be heard.

Jack wraps his right arm around Abelia's back, his fingertips feeling her ribs. She rests her left hand on his upper arm, giving him her other hand. The acoustic guitar is now mixed with recorder notes, to which he straightens his upper body. He remains in place, shifting his weight from one leg to the other a few times. Abelia senses the changes and does the same.

Then the melancholy song begins and he takes a small step backwards. Abelia follows his step a little too quickly at first, then follows with the other leg after a slight delay. A step to the left follows and he leads her into a back ocho. To do this he leads her into a half turn on the spot, takes a step to the right, which she follows, then the same turn in the opposite direction.

Now he becomes unsure for a moment. He signals with his upper body to step aside, but doesn't do it. Abelia is about to take the step when she notices. She skilfully turns the step into an embellishment by circling her foot over the floor and then stopping.

Jack now offers her a tighter embrace, leaning his upper body slightly forwards. She accepts and presses her breasts against him. He embraces her back completely. She slides her left hand up his upper arm and hugs him over her shoulder. Her fingertips touch the nape of his neck. She feels the movement right above her chest. They dance a few turns, then stop and do some simple ornaments. During these phases, Abelia can feel Jack's heartbeat. She nestles her face against his neck, willingly surrendering to his guidance.

The song becomes more powerful and this is transferred to both of them. Their dance doesn't speed up, but their movements become more intense. They interpret the deep melancholy in the song with steps and movements that are fast at first and then become slower and slower, as if they are gliding through honey that sweetly and viscously takes the tempo out of them.

Jack feels her breath on his neck, like a damp mist that leaves a soft fog on the mirror in the heat. A fog on which words and signs can be written with bare fingers. Words and signs that are only meant for this moment, until the fog dissolves again.

A guitar solo kicks in, adding to the already high intensity. Now they move faster, a turn, another turn, then back to the other side. He leads her leg around his. She wraps her leg around his thigh, remains in this position for a moment and then releases herself again after touching his neck with her lips for a brief moment.

A few more dynamic movements follow in the never-ending build up to the song. With their upper bodies pressed tightly together, Jack releases the embrace for a moment to enable Abelia to move in his arms.

The song comes to an end. Jack anticipates this and reduces the tempo. From the turns, he again performs some ornaments on the spot. Abelia follows all the time without knowing exactly what these figures are. She just dances without thinking or worrying, just living this one moment.

Their bodies are now drenched in sweat, their faces flushed. The intensity wanes, their bodies relax as their movements slow down, until the song finally fades out and they stand in front of each other in an intimate embrace.

They feel each other's warm, moist breath and the salty film that has settled on their skin in the last few minutes. They stay in this embrace for a while, without moving, without saying a word. They feel their hearts beating like a rhythmic drumming, which starts loud and steady and then decreases in volume and tempo just as steadily.

9

They sit facing each other in silence, each lost in its own thoughts. The music echoes, like an endless refrain on a continuous loop, silent yet piercing. The atmosphere in the compartment is heated, like a jungle after a long tropical downpour.

Jack sees himself dancing with Abelia once again, it seems surreal. He can sense her movements and once again feels the dynamics in the turns, how they have increased until the dance culminates in an intimate embrace.

Abelia stares thoughtfully into space. 'What have I just done?' she asks herself, smiling. She is filled with a little shame, but no regrets.

"How did you feel about the dance?" he asks, looking into her eyes.

She turns her head towards him and meets his gaze. "I didn't know I could dance like that. You lead really well."

"No, you dance well," he insists in a firm voice.

"I've never danced like this before. I'm surprised at myself," she says, smiling to herself.

"In some places we had our friction points. But when we allowed them and improvised over them, the dance became perfect," says Jack thoughtfully.

"Maybe the only reason we dance so well is because we dance together. The harmony between us is so great that it comes out in the dance."

"I want to dance a much more with you."

"As much as you want," she says with a contented sigh.

Abelia sits down opposite him, taking off her shoes and resting her feet on his thighs. Then she leans back and follows his gaze outside, his hands cupping her ankles. She snuggles deep into the seat and hums a tune Jack has never heard before.

A motorway runs parallel to the tracks. There are a few lorries on the road, driving at a leisurely pace. Cars are passing the lorries all the time, some overtaking at extremely high speed. Sometimes the cars form small convoys as they pass. The first car speeds past the lorries in the left-hand lane, followed closely by three cars. As if on a race track, the cars behind them drive up impatiently and close together, as if they had already lapped the car in front. Then the car in front finally moves to the right and the car behind tries to overtake, which it only manages with difficulty. The cars behind start to tailgate. They drive even closer to assert their claim to the lead. The overtaken car does not give up and follows the convoy to tailgate.

An animal transporter loaded with pigs is driving parallel to the train. The animals stand close together and look out.

Jack watches as the pigs stick their flat noses up in the air, as if they want to catch a last breath of fresh air or smell the scent of freedom before their final journey to the factory.

"When I see that, I don't want to eat meat anymore," says Abelia, shaking her head.

"Especially pork," says Jack, surprised at the irony sharpness he hadn't intended.

She looks at him sternly, then turns back to the transporter. "It's terrible how the animals have to suffer. They are only born to be slaughtered at some point. Then they are fattened up as fast as possible to get fat. Of course, they are not allowed to run around, otherwise it takes longer for them to reach the fattening maturity. After a very short time they have the weight of a full-grown pig and are taken to the slaughterhouse."

"Nature has made murderers out of all of us, vegetarians excluded," Jack says as he looks at the animals.

"At least we're accomplices, because we demand the meat. Just because we're too lazy to change our eating habits.

"However, I'm not prepared to change my behaviour. I don't want to go against something that corresponds to my nature. It would be like trying to override a part of evolution."

"What exactly do you mean?" she asks, her eyebrows raised.

"It was only when humans started eating meat that their development accelerated and they were able to overtake the other animals. Brains got bigger and there was more energy available. If humans hadn't started eating meat, we probably wouldn't be here together. Perhaps we would still be living in caves, or we would have died out because other carnivores would have overtaken us and wiped us out."

"That's rubbish," she says with reddened cheeks. "You can't seriously think that meat eaters are the more intelligent people. I've never heard such nonsense."

"That's not even my own opinion. These are scientific findings that have even been proven. Without meat, humans would not have evolved in the way they did. Even today, it is not possible to give up meat without suffering long-term damage."

"What kind of damage is that supposed to do?" she replies, laughing mockingly. "No heart attack, no fatty liver, no high cholesterol," she adds with a sarcastic laugh.

"Meat is like many other things. Too much is not good, it's even dangerous. It can make us sick and kill us. Whether it's meat, the daily glass of wine or sometimes even love."

"So you think love will kill us?"

"I don't think love will necessarily kill us. But too much love can kill."

"Then why are we sitting here together if it's so dangerous?"

"I'm not talking about us," Jack says reassuringly.

"Oh, right, there's no danger of too much love here, so everything's fine. That means we just have to make sure it's not too much love, then everything will be fine," she says snappishly, crossing her arms and turning away.

Biting his lip, Jack gazes into Abelia's dark eyes as they stare at him from the side. He thinks how beautiful and mysterious she can be, but also how frightening at this moment. Finally, he takes a deep breath and continues: "Surely you can remember your first great love."

"Yes, of course."

"I'm sure you remember the pain when you broke up."

"I cried for nights."

"And what was it like after the second failed relationship?"

"At least I didn't cry as much then."

"This is exactly what I mean. Imagine if feelings were always this extreme. That's how it is with some people. They go completely crazy."

"I think something is going crazy with you, but at least now I understand what you mean," she says, trying to suppress a grin, which she doesn't manage.

The animal transporter with the pigs is still driving parallel to the train. A car is overtaking it at a leisurely pace, while two other cars are approaching from behind at high speed. They don't slow down, don't even seem to take their foot off the accelerator. They take their chance and drive up to the overtaking car at high speed until the last moment, then brake so late that they almost seem to touch.

The overtaking car continues unimpressed at a constant speed, and when it has overtaken the van and is back in the right-hand lane, the other two accelerate and drive off as fast as they came.

The van slows down and turns right into the exit and disappears after a bend.

10

They sit there in silence for a while. The cherries and the box with the cherry pits are still on the table. The pits are arranged like a pyramid, shimmering bright red in the fading sunlight.

They pass wide fields, then some pastures where cows are grazing peacefully, watching impassively at the passing train. Jack wonders what the cows are thinking as the train passes them. Do they even understand what a train is, and can they imagine what it's like to be on a journey?

Then they approach a farm where a few horses are standing in an enclosure. They were all looking in the same direction, as if waiting for something.

"Look how beautiful they are," Abelia says in a rapturous tone.

"Beautiful animals," he replies sincerely. He reflects on the fact that he has never had much of a thing for horses. But he finds these horses truly beautiful. They gleam in the warm light of the sun, which makes them look even more impressive.

"I had a horse once," Abelia says, her eyes shining.

"Oh, really?"

"Yes, a black horse. He was my pride and joy. He was so strong and sublime, and incredibly loyal."

"What happened to the horse?"

"We sold him when I started studying. I couldn't take care of him anymore, so there was no point."

"I'm sure it wasn't easy for you to give it away."

"It was the worst time in my life up to that point. If I had known beforehand how much it would hurt, I would probably have given up studying. At that time I had no idea about pain and what was to come."

"How old were you when you got the horse?"

"I was fifteen and my school report looked pretty bad, at least as far as my parents' expectations were concerned. They said that if I improved my average by two grades, I'd get a horse. So I studied like crazy for six months and finished the school year with top marks."

He looks at Abelia, gazes into her shining eyes and listens to her talk without really noticing a word. She has so many traits that he has come to love. She seems proud, triumphant and at the same time so sensitive that it touches him.

She talks and he smiles, she describes with gestures and he nods. He feels a sense of contentment that he hasn't felt for a long time.

But the pauses between her sentences become longer and longer. Like a broken engine, it announces itself with a stutter, and then it doesn't take long for the engine to come to a complete stop. Just like that stuttering engine, she stops talking and just looks out of the window.

Jack thinks about what to ask, but can't think of anything. All the possible questions he could ask about horses are running through his head. But either he already knows the answer, or he's not really interested. He toys with the idea of asking a question, just to get her to keep talking.

The shining in her eyes is gone. The bright joy of life has given way to a dark dejection. But he can't think of a question that would make her light up again.

He looks at her for a long time, and the features that were proud and radiant a moment ago have given way to an expressionlessness, even a disgruntlement that makes him sad. He takes the appointment diary out of his jacket and leafs through it. He flicks through page after page without really looking at the contents. He turns the pages slowly and steadily, almost as if they were dancing to the beat.

When he reaches the end, he randomly opens it again in the middle. He reads the lines he left behind and can't remember why he wrote them.

Then he looks up at Abelia, who is staring at the appointment diary with a stone-faced expression. She doesn't blink, no facial muscles show any movement. She just fixes her gaze on the diary.

Jack puts it aside and turns to her. "Are you all right?"

"Yeah," she says without looking at him.

"Really?" he asks quietly.

"Yes, everything's fine," she says a little louder, which sounds louder than it is because of his soft voice.

They sit in silence. The air feels as thick as if they were immersed in a dark, dense fog. Jack can't look her in the eyes in this moment. Every time he looks at her, he reflexively averts his gaze. He feels how far away she is at this moment, in the unreachable distance. As she sits there, cold and distant, he feels a pang of pain and is overcome by a mixture of loneliness and helplessness.

He looks out again, scratches his head and, with a clumsy arm movement, bumps into the box of cherry pits, which threatens to tip over as if in slow motion. He tries to hold it with his hand, but this only energises the box, sending it flying off the table in a high arc. The cherry pits spread all over the floor, hissing softly.

Abelia turns her head and looks at the cherry pits scattered around the room without moving her body, shaking her head.

"Sorry," he says sheepishly, sweeping the pits into a corner with his hands.

"They could have been disposed of earlier," she says, helping him by pushing some of the pits into another corner with her feet.

When the pits are scattered in the corners, she looks out at the landscape again. Jack looks at his hands, black from the dirt on the floor.

"I'm going to wash my hands," he says quietly and stands up.

She nods expressionlessly and he pushes himself out the door.

He walks down the corridor as if in a dream. The surrounding sounds are muffled and he feels nauseous.

He hurries almost at a run to the toilet, pulls open the door and enters quickly, only to close it behind him immediately. As if he were on the run, he breathes a sigh of relief and pauses for a moment. He wants to turn around, but he can't let go of the door. His vision is blurred, the room is spinning. He held on to the door, the nausea so intense that he feels like he is going to vomit. He breaks out in a cold sweat, his knees start to tremble, his breathing gets harder. He wonders what is happening to him, searching for a logical explanation, but finds none.

Thoughts flash through his mind every second. Abelia as she talks and laughs, followed by Rob as he intrusively turns to her. Then the conductor punching out the tickets, and finally he sees the suffering dogs.

Then he loses consciousness.

11

A cherry pit has pressed itself into the sole of Abelia's shoe. She kicks it away angrily. There are still a few pits scattered across the floor. Some still have the shiny, moist flesh stuck to them, others are grey from the dirt that covers them.

She looks at the seat where Jack has just been sitting. She notices some stains, probably from the cherry pits, but they don't really seem strange. It seems like a pattern that belongs there. Sighing, she turns her head and gazes aimlessly outside. A housing estate of tall concrete blocks passes by. Crows are making a mess of the overflowing rubbish bins in front of the houses.

A tear escapes from her eye and runs slowly down her cheek, leaving a wet trail on her face.

There is so much she wants to share, so much she needs to tell. But she can't. When she tries to talk about her emotions, she feels as if she is standing in front of a cold wall that bounces her own words back at her like an echo. There is no sound behind the wall, everything is muffled. It laughs coldly back at her and leaves her alone with herself.

She thinks about who has ever really listened to her and shakes her head. No one in her relationships has ever really listened to her. As different as Jack is from her ex-boyfriend Brian, there is this one thing in common that makes her so infinitely sad.

Was the other woman really the worst thing that happened to her in this relationship, or was it just a logical consequence of all the little things that didn't fit?

It seems like it was only yesterday that she caught Brian with the other woman.

She came home, unlocked the door and immediately realised that something was wrong. In the hallway everything was as usual, but instinctively she went into the living room. There were two half-full glasses of wine and lipstick on one of them. As if in a trance, she walked towards the bedroom, where she could already hear noises coming from inside. She knew exactly what was going to happen next, but she couldn't decide or do anything else. She had to see for herself, there was no alternative. As if hypnotised, she opened the door and saw Brian lying naked in bed. A woman was bent over him, moving lustfully on top of him. His hands were clutching her breasts.

Abelia remembers opening her mouth wide. She wanted to scream, but she couldn't, no sound came out. She put her hand over her mouth, tears streaming down her cheeks. Crying silently, she went back into the living room, took a big red felt-tip pen and a piece of paper. With the pen she wrote the words: "You'll be out of here by twelve o'clock tomorrow. If not, my brothers will come and take over."

The next day she came home just after noon and he was gone. He didn't leave anything and he didn't call.

Not a word was left.

She never knew if he regretted it or missed her. He was just gone, as if nothing mattered, as if she didn't matter.

Maybe it was her own fault. After all, she was the one who had drifted away from him. But why she did it, he obviously never was interested in. Not once did he ask her how she was feeling.

Even when he forgot her birthday and came home drunk as a skunk. She had been looking forward to a nice evening with him, so she sat at the dinner table in silence and waited. She waited a long time. Late at night he came in and wasn't at all surprised that she was still up and sitting at the table. When she spoke to him about it, he even got angry. Abelia was angry too, and wanted to confront him about what he had been up to, but he was stronger.

The fist in her face felt like a huge wooden hammer, knocking her to the ground. She didn't cry a tear, she didn't want to show him any weakness at that moment. No, he didn't get that. She stood up with trembling knees, her face felt hot, a stabbing pain burned through her jawbone, but she didn't show it. She stood up straight in front of Brian, looked him deep in the eyes and grinned. He was furious and shouted at her that it was her own fault for provoking him like that. She didn't say a word, just stood there grinning. He shouted even louder and asked if she hadn't had enough yet, but she just stood there and grinned. Then he grabbed her with both hands and pushed her over a glass side table. The table toppled over, the glass shattered and a shard pierced her leg. As she braced herself with her hand, she heard a crack in her wrist. Her body felt like it had been run over by a truck. She took a deep breath, got to her feet and stood in front of Brian again, grinning. Startled, he stared at her bloodied leg, still pierced by the shard in it. He bent down to her leg, but she backed away, stopped and continued to grin. He took another step towards her and she stepped back without breaking her grin.

"You're crazy," he said, and left the apartment.

She didn't even think the fact that he had hit her was the worst part. She found it much worse that he came home the next day and acted as if nothing had happened. Not once that day did he ask her how she was. This indifference hurt her more than anything else.

She was all the happier when she met Jack. A reliable and honest man with whom she felt safe.

She also liked that he opened up to her. His helplessness when she talked to Rob touched her deeply, so that at this point there was no more doubt in her mind.

Jack and Brian only have one thing in common. They are so preoccupied with themselves that they don't notice each other. Jack was interested in so many things, but he always stayed on the surface. He never made the effort to get through to her, to find out the story about Brian that she would have loved to tell him.

She wonders if all men have these characteristics or if she just attracts a certain type of man. Or maybe it's just her and she wonders what she might have done wrong.

Abelia looks out and watches the sun as it moves down from the sky, illuminating her face warmly and comfortingly.

12

Jack comes to and sees the sink and toilet in front of him. He lies curled up against the door and tries to remember what happened. All he can remember is that he felt nauseous and then lost consciousness. He wonders what time it is and how long he's been lying there, but he has no idea.

He looks at his hands, which are black with dirt. He struggles to get up, goes to the sink and begins to wash each finger. He rubs his hands with plenty of soap. The lather of the soap spreads and slowly dissolves the dirt. Then he rinses his hands and the black water runs down the drain. There seems to be no end to the dirt, and although the soap dissolves the dirt, his hands remain dark. He soaps his hands again, rubs them together and rinses them, and again the black water runs down the drain without the dirt coming off his hands. He repeats the process a few more times. He rubs his now reddened hands with increasingly frantic movements. Finally he succeeds. The soap is working and the water is getting clearer and clearer until the dirt has disappeared from his hands. He looks in disbelief at his fingers, now completely clean and smelling of soap. He stands up, leans on the sink and looks in the mirror.

"You look a little tired," he says tonelessly to his reflection, looking at the small wrinkles around his eyes. Then he discovers a dark stain on his chin. He turns the tap back on and takes some soap to wash the stain away. It seems to him that he is increasing the size of the stain rather than removing it. Then he grabs some paper towels, which laid out to dry hands. The towels feel like rough sandpaper. Jack presses and rubs vigorously over the stain. Little by little, the dark stain disappears. What remains is a dark red spot caused by the intense friction of the paper towels. He strokes his fingers over the spot but feels nothing, everything feels smooth.

Then, slightly dazed, he walks back along the corridor towards the compartment, stops at a window and looks out.

The window pane is full of streaks and greasy fingerprints. In some places, the smears are so large and dense that the pane looks like frosted glass and he can only see dimly through it. Jack opens the window by pulling it down hard. It gives way noisily, and a cold draft immediately flows in. He takes a deep breath of the cold wind, which blows refreshingly into his face.

The sun is already low and approaching the horizon. Its light is fading and makes the landscape look as if it is bathed in artificial light. A few cumulus clouds can be seen in the sky, which seem to stand still, like in an impressionist painting by Monet.

A group of motorcyclists are riding at a relaxed pace along a country road. Two of them ride side by side at the front, the others follow at a short distance. They form a V-shape, like a flock of birds on their way to warmer regions in autumn. Far to the south, to escape the cold.

He closes the window and returns to the compartment.

Abelia is sitting there, just as she was when he left the compartment. She is looking out without paying any attention to him. Her posture is upright and straight, her arms crossed across her chest. Her head is slightly raised, making her neck look even slimmer and more graceful.

He enters and sneaks quietly to his seat. She takes no notice of him, not even when he sits opposite her again and looks at her. Her gaze remains fixed on the outside, without the slightest movement, not even the slightest twitch in her face. She sits there as if she is in another world, far away from the here and now.

The sun dips into the horizon in a golden yellow. The last rays of light enter the compartment frontally and illuminate it colourfully. The warmth of the light caresses their faces. Jack lays his head back and holds his face up to the light to catch the last rays of the sun. The deep blue sky is streaked with a yellow glow. The scattered clouds glow a fiery red, like wrought iron lying in the hot embers, waiting to be moulded into shape.

Gradually, the deep red colour gives way to darkness. The sun begins to dissolve, as if by itself, even before it finally disappears behind the horizon. The glow on the horizon diminishes by the moment, the sky becomes darker and darker, until finally the first lights appear on the streets and in the houses take centre stage, heralding the night.

Their eyes meet in the window, reflected in the falling night. Abelia looks through him as if he were not there. Her gaze is still directed into nothingness, without any movement.

It is difficult for him to look into her eyes. His eyes twitch reflexively every time he looks into hers, as if she might catch him doing something illicit, forbidden.

He longs for her shining eyes, the way they smile at him warmly and happily. But she seems so far away that he is not sure if he will ever see this woman again who has so enchanted him.

13

A loud screech echoes through the carriage. A jolt is sensed and the train reduces its speed sharply. Abelia is pushed back into her seat and Jack has to brace himself with his hands to keep from falling forward onto her.

They remain like this until the train comes to a halt.

It is deadly silent, time seems to freeze for a moment. Nothing can be heard. No voices, no coughing or clearing of throats, but no complaining either.

"What was that?" Abelia asks after a few seconds.

"That was an emergency stop." He peers out, his head close to the window, looking out behind to see if he can make out anything that might have caused the emergency stop. Nothing is visible in the darkness, all he can see is the night and Abelia reflected in the windscreen.

"Something must have happened," she says, almost in a whisper.

"Maybe a suicide."

Now she looks in that direction too, eyes narrowed, but she can't recognise anything either.

"Can you see anything?" she asks.

Jack presses his head against the window and shakes his head: "It's all black."

The carriage becomes restless, footsteps and voices are audible. Passengers come out of the compartments and scurry along the corridor. Some are talking, others are asking questions and listening intently to the people analysing the braking process and discussing possible causes.

"I've seen it all before," says a medium-sized, corpulent man, waving his hand. "I've witnessed a suicide like that twice, and each time I missed my train connection, those damn suicides. It's not just what they do to the train driver, those idiots. A lot of people are late for work because of that scumbag."

"Well, people are more likely to be off work at this time of night," says a voice from the background.

The corpulent man's head reddens, the colour rising to his high forehead. "And what about the people who are out on the night shift?" he snorts. "Besides, there are enough people out of work where their families are waiting and worrying. I can list a few more reasons. Nobody's here because they're bored, I can guarantee that."

"Now let's wait and see. Maybe it's not a suicide," says the man in the background.

"It's definitely one, I can assure you of that. I've had enough experience of that. I've had an idiot like that in front of the locomotive twice."

"Geeentlemen, please return to your seats," the conductor calls through the corridor. Grumbling, the first passengers return to their seats.

"Hey conductor, some idiot jumped in front of the train again," the corpulent man shouts to the conductor.

"Please return to your seat. It will soon become clear why the train has stopped," the conductor says impassively, stopping in front of the corpulent man and making an inviting gesture towards his seat.

"Leave it, conductor, I know my way around ..."

"Would you like to go to your seat immediately?" the conductor interrupts him in a sharp tone, standing directly in front of the man and looking down at him.

"It's alright, I'll go," the corpulent man replies and goes to his seat without saying another word. The conductor watches him until he is seated, then walks on, shaking his head. As he passes Jack and Abelia's compartment, he glances in from the corner of his eye, stops and half opens the door. "So, is everything all right with you two?"

"We're fine. Has something happened?" asks Abelia.

"It could well be that someone made a joke, unfortunately that happens quite often," says the conductor in a calm, almost fatherly voice.

"It would be nice if it was just a joke, although I'm not much for that kind of humour," says Abelia.

"I'm sure it will clear up quickly. As soon as I know more, I'll let you know."

Smiling mildly, the conductor closes the door and walks away at a brisk pace. Shortly afterwards, they hear him directing the next passengers to their seats.

A blue light can be seen in the distance, illuminating the darkness at a steady pace. The flashing light gets closer, then a police car can be seen. More police cars follow, approaching the train in a long line. The flashing blue lights of the cars merge into a diffuse flicker.

Several ambulances can now be seen, followed by the fire brigade. The sirens are sounding and the shrill wailing seems to be coming from everywhere, getting louder and louder.

The sky flickers in a piercing play of colours, interspersed with the blue lights of the emergency vehicles. The sirens become so loud that Jack gets an oppressive feeling in his chest. He looks at Abelia, who is watching the scene intently. Her gaze seems calm, but her facial muscles are tense.

Most of the vehicles stop at the front of the locomotive, some drive to the rear and position themselves at the end of the train. A police car stops in front of their carriage, and two policemen quickly get out and search the area. Abelia watches them curiously. The flickering blue light shines rhythmically into her face.

A white light shines from the end of the train outside. Jack looks out and sees large floodlights brightly illuminating a square. He can't see everything, it's too far away and the visibility is too limited.

"Can you see anything?" he asks, without looking at Abelia.

"Just light," she says quietly, looking up at the spotlights, which spread brightly across her face. The moist shine of her eyes reflects the bright light, accompanied by the colourful flickering of the blue lights.

More vehicles approach the train. A never-ending spectacle of wailing sirens, flashing lights and hectic movement takes place outside. Police officers walk alongside the train, illuminating the area with torches. One of the policemen bends down underneath the carriage and shines his torch thoroughly and purposefully over the tracks.

The policeman straightens up and suddenly shines his torch directly into Jack's face. Startled, he looks into the glaring light, which blinds him so badly that he feels a sharp pain. He squints his eyes, holds a hand protectively in front of his face and turns his head to the side.

"He must be crazy," says Abelia, straightening up and looking at the policeman with furrowed brows. He shines with his torch in her face, but she doesn't move. She braves the blinding light and looks the policeman straight in the eye. He lowers the torch and looks at her. Their eyes meet and, like two fighters, they wrestle, with the aim to knocking the other down.

The policeman now lowers his gaze, turns and walks briskly away. Abelia looks after him triumphantly, then turns her gaze gently to Jack, who is watching the policeman walk away.

The sound of footsteps can be heard in the corridor again. Policemen cross the carriage at a fast pace. Two of the policemen stop in front of the compartment, look inside and open the door. One of them is tall and slim. He is wearing a grey suit, a hat and a trench coat. He looks like he has stepped out of an Edgar Wallace thriller. The second policeman is a good head shorter, also wearing a suit and an anorak over it. His thinning hair is greasy, which makes him look unkempt.

They enter the compartment and take a big step forward.

"Sorry to disturb you," says the man in the trench coat. "I'm Inspector Hartmann and this is my colleague Hempel. We need to ask you some questions."

They look up at the inspector. He takes his time to look at each of them in turn. There is no blinking in his gaze, he seeks eye contact directly and without hesitation. He seems determined to bore his gaze directly into their memories.

A few seconds pass before the inspector asks in a firm voice, "Where have you been for the last hour?"

"We've been here," Jack replies curtly.

"You've been here without interruption for the last sixty minutes?" Hempel insists, looking like an inconspicuous supporting actor.

"Yes, we've been here the whole time," Jack says in a calm voice.

The officers then turn to Abelia, who looks at them calmly, one by one.

"Do you have anything to add?" asks Hempel.

"No," she says laconically, looking at him calmly.

Hempel fixes his gaze on Abelia, then looks at Jack. "Are you quite sure?" he asks in a harsh tone, standing threateningly next to his colleague Hartmann.

"Yes," Jack says, avoiding the officer's gaze.

"We'll come and see you again. Please don't leave the compartment," Hartmann says.

Without waiting for a word, they go out and close the door, which bangs shut. Then they walk away with a firm step.

Jack looks at Abelia, who averts her eyes. He observes her soft, relaxed features and her determined expression at the same time. He tries to read a thought in her face, but he can't make anything out. She is like a mysterious book whose contents he does not know.

"Thank you," he says, almost in a whisper.

"There is nothing to thank you for," she replies in a quiet tone, without looking at him.

Not sure if they both mean the same thing, Jack thinks about the way she answered him. Only now does he realise what she knows about him, and to what extent he might be at her mercy. But that doesn't worry him. He wonders why, but he can't explain it. On the contrary, he feels light and, in a way, unassailable. No one has ever known so much about him.

He is grateful that he has been able to share his secret with her. He has no doubt that it is in good hands with her. He has great confidence in her, even though he is not sure how well he knows her.

But he also realises how one-sided it is. She knows his secret and therefore his deepest abysses. He, on the other hand, knows nothing about her abysses. And yet he feels he knows everything about her. She has told him so much, and yet nothing. He doesn't know what it's like deep inside her soul.

He wonders whether it would make a difference if she knew less about him, whether she would like him more. He dismisses the thought again as he sees the picture outside start to move. There is a jolt, then the train moves backwards. At walking speed, it rolls almost silently towards the headlights. The picture outside changes like a scene change in a theatre, as if the next act were waiting for them. The brightly lit square comes closer and closer.

14

With each approach, the contours of the place become clearer and clearer. Everything seems to get bigger with each passing moment. Then they reach the level of the place and the train comes to a halt.

The compartment is brightly lit by the glaring headlights. Jack looks out over the square, where police officers are marking off crime scenes and ambulance staff are looking around. In the middle of the square lies a body covered by a white sheet, which Jack does not immediately notice. Only after looking at it for a while does he realise that it is a dead body. Abelia doesn't recognise the corpse either, and jerks back in horror when she realises what it is.

The body is not completely covered. Part of the head is visible from the side, and an arm sticks out from under the sheet. The hand is open, as if trying to grasp something. The arm is covered with blood. The blood runs across the skin in different shades of red, like a watercolour pattern. There is a large, dry wound in the middle of the arm, on which scabs have formed.

"I can't believe it," Abelia says.

"What do you mean?" asks Jack, without taking his eyes off the body.

"Don't you recognise him?"

He looks at the body. He recognises hair that, like the bloodied arm, is not completely covered by the sheet. Not all of it is bloody, so he can see that it is blonde hair, long blonde hair.

"Who do you think it is?" he asks.

"He looks like Rob, don't you remember? The mountain climber who was in our compartment."

"How do you think he got there? He would have had to overtake the train somehow after getting off to throw himself in front of it. That's impossible, nobody can be that fast."

"I know that's actually impossible, but he looks like this. Look at the hair and the graze on his forearm. That looks just like him."

"It could be him, but it could also be someone else. I can't even tell if it's a man or a woman. It could be practically anyone with blonde hair. The graze could have come from anywhere, pure coincidence. It could also have happened on impact."

"Something tells me it's him," Abelia says, shaking her head.

"Okay, let's assume he is. Let's also assume that he wanted to throw himself in front of this train. But there are a few questions that are a bit unclear. How could he get past us so quickly after getting off and then jump in front of the train? He would have needed a helicopter to do that. Even if he had managed it, why would he do it? Why would he choose this train of all trains? There's no reason at all, trains run all the time, all over the country."

"I don't know," Abelia says thoughtfully. "All I know is that he looks like Rob."

They stare hypnotised at the dead body, no longer wanting to look, but unable to look away. They barely notice the flickering blue light. It is just a dull flash that comes and goes. They also no longer perceive the headlights as glaring and dazzling. They just look at the body.

The compartment door opens and Inspector Hartmann enters, closely followed by Hempel. They face Jack directly and looking down at him arrogantly. They appear aggressive and superior as they scrutinise him with conspiratorial knowledge. Inspector Hartmann has one hand in the pocket of his trench coat, with the other he is pointing at Jack, his index finger pointing menacingly like the barrel of a gun. Hempel stands beside him, grinning confidently, with an unmistakable trace of malicious glee.

"You said you were in the compartment all the time," Hartmann says in an exaggeratedly calm tone.

Jack looks up at him and doesn't say a word. He is getting hot, he feels the tingling heat spreading through his body and finally reaching his head. His face flushes, his throat tightens and he can only look up at the men without saying a word. Hartmann is still pointing his finger, Hempel is grinning happily beside him.

"Have you lost your tongue?" asks Hartmann in an attacking tone that Jack barely notices.

"What are you trying to say?" Abelia interjects, drawing attention to herself. The officers now turn their attention to her, causing Jack to sigh with relief.

"Your partner was seen by other guests outside the compartment," says Hempel, still grinning.

"So what?" she replies.

"That means you didn't tell us the truth earlier. You claimed he was in the compartment the whole time, which obviously wasn't the case."

"He was there the whole time. If he was away for a short time, that can't be the problem. What are you accusing him of anyway?"

The officers don't answer, looking at each other, then at Jack, who feels caught and exposed.

"How long were you outside the compartment?" Hartmann asks in a conciliatory tone.

"I was only in the toilet for a short time, maybe five minutes," he says.

"Why didn't you say so before?" Hempel follows up.

Jack looks up wordlessly, his throat tightening again. He feels like a beaten boxer, backed into a corner, at the mercy of his opponent's fists. Feeling the hail of blows, unable to defend himself.

Inspector Hartmann turns to Abelia, who is looking calmly past him with her arms crossed.

"Very well," he says. "We'll get back to you." He casts a threatening glance back at Jack, then turns and walks away. Hempel, still grinning, follows wordlessly.

They are watching the events in the place in silence. Police officers are still walking around with torches, although the square is so well lit that the surroundings appear as bright as day.

Meanwhile, a hearse had arrived. The undertakers are standing together with the emergency doctor, talking emotionlessly.

"Why are the police asking so many questions?" asks Abelia. Jack looks at her wordlessly and sighs helplessly. Then she looks him straight in the eye, leans forward and takes his hands.

"We shouldn't tell them anything more," she says, looking at him insistently.

"You're right, it's probably for the best," he replies and feels the warmth in her gaze.

At this moment, he feels an unconditional bond. He looks into her warm eyes for a long time, gazing gently at him, and feels her hands holding his hand tightly.

The conductor's voice can be heard again. He is talking to some of the passengers, his words sound reassuring. They can't hear what he's saying, but he seems to be getting closer. Then he passes their compartment, nods in a friendly way and walks past them. Then he thinks for a moment, stops, takes a few steps back and opens the door.

"Well, is everything all right with you?"

"Do you know when it will continue?" asks Abelia without answering his question.

"Yes, it leaves in a few minutes, don't need to worry."

"What are the police wanting on the train?"

"Well," the conductor stammers, searching for words. They look at him expectantly.

He pauses for a moment and thinks, looking around somewhat helplessly, until he finally continues in a whisper: "You know, the door to our carriage was open and according to the police, there are indications that the dead man came from our train."

"How can that be?" asks Abelia sceptically.

"He must have jumped out of the open door during the journey," he says quietly, turning around briefly as if to make sure no one can hear anything. Then he leans down to them. "The police suspect he was pushed out."

"Do the police have any particular suspicions yet?" Jack asks, his voice trembling.

"No, not that I know of. They've questioned a few people here, but apparently without any concrete suspicions."

The conductor smiles at Jack, small wrinkles forming in his eyes. Then he looks at his watch and whistles through his teeth in surprise.

"Well, I have to get going now. Make yourself comfortable and don't worry too much. You'll be home soon."

"Thanks," Jack says, but the conductor says nothing. He just turns for a moment and winks at him.

Outside, the undertakers place a coffin next to the deceased and talk emotionlessly. They are all wearing the same black suits, white shirts and black ties. Jack and Abelia watch the proceedings intently, hoping to recognise something more when the body is placed in the coffin. The undertakers line up in front of the lifeless body, one on each side. But now the train continues its journey, slowly rolling forward.

The undertakers move as if in slow motion, while the train inexorably picks up speed. The scenery moves away faster and faster. Now the undertakers bend down to grab the corpse, moving further and further away.

"I can't see anything," Abelia says in a desperate voice.

"Neither can I," Jack replies resignedly.

Now the undertakers heave the corpse up, the sheet slips, but nothing more can be seen than the blonde hair. Then the train takes a bend and the place with the dead body, the vehicles and the emergency services disappears for good. The image of this scene has disappeared as suddenly as a bad dream that dissolves into nothingness after a long, restless night.

15

The monotonous rolling sound of the train has filled the room again. Jack relaxes and listens to this sound that is so familiar to him.

The thoughts in his head dissolve like soap bubbles in which the images are reflected. They burst into a thousand pieces as if they had never been there.

Meanwhile, Abelia leans back in the cushion and looks out thoughtfully. She doesn't look worried, nor does she seem particularly concerned. She is simply looking out, her eyes fixed on the darkness.

The peaceful expression on Abelia's face and the soothing sound of the train give Jack a deep sense of peace that he hasn't felt for a long time. He feels a pleasant heaviness and finally tiredness overcomes him. Deeply relaxed, he sinks back into his seat and closes his eyes.

He is standing in a large square, looking down at himself. He is wearing a perfectly fitting black suit. His tie is tied in a festive knot. It is very tight, so that he can feel the pressure on his neck. All around him are fairground stalls, merry-go-rounds and food stands. Everything glows brightly and colourfully in the darkness. Loud music comes from a Ferris wheel. Children are running around, screaming and laughing. A clown walks by, holding a bunch of balloons that stretch high into the sky.

He notices Abelia standing at the Ferris wheel with a ticket. She gets into a gondola on her own and the ride begins as soon as she sits down. Her eyes are wet and a tear runs down her cheek. Swaying, the gondola starts to move and takes Abelia up into the sky. Jack can see her sad face, every detail ... he wants to call her, but he has no voice.

Then he hears a screech coming from a maze. It is a house full of glass walls through which the visitor must find his way. He goes to the ticket office, buys a ticket and enters the maze. Without thinking, he moves in as if guided by someone else's hand. He follows a long glass corridor. He can no longer make out anything outside. All he can see are glass walls and mirrors bathed in a dark light.

He feels his way through the corridors, hands first. Left, then right, then left again. He has long since lost his bearings and has no idea how long he has been in this place. He follows the corridor, changing direction again and again, until he finally reaches the dead end and can go no further.

A large mirror stands there as a finishing touch, and he looks at his reflection. He sees himself in the suit with the tie and the white shirt. He discovers a red stain on the shirt, but cannot identify what it is. His face in the mirror looks old and wrinkled. His eyes are black, looking at him blankly and without expression. Startled, he averts his gaze and turns around.

He finds another corridor through which he winds his way until he reaches a large hall of mirrors.

All around him, his reflection looks back at him, but it is not the same image every time. In one mirror he sees himself laughing, in another he stands there screaming with his mouth wide open. Sharp fangs, like those of a predator, glint at him. In yet another mirror he crouches in solitude, lost in himself, sobbing.

Jack turns away, but wherever he turns, he faces a different reflection every time. He feels dizzy, the room seems to be spinning. The floor begins to move and coordination becomes increasingly difficult.

He can barely stand on his feet when suddenly two hands grab his neck from behind. He takes a big step forwards and turns round when he sees a figure rushing towards him. It looks like a mythical creature, half human, half animal.

The head is oversized, but the figure has no face. Long blond hair hangs down, it is unkempt and shaggy. The whole body is covered with thick fur.

The creature approaches him, raises its claws, grabs his neck and presses him against a mirror. Jack grabs the creature's neck with his hands and squeezes as well. He feels his breath catch in his throat. His throat is crushed by the powerful claws. He continues to squeeze the creature's neck tighter and tighter with his hands.

They are standing opposite each other, fighting for their lives, and he realises that only one of them will survive. He can no longer breathe and panic rises through him. He senses that he is about to pass out. With the last of his strength, he squeezes his hands together and presses his thumbs deep into the creature's throat. His knees go weak and he feels that he will soon lose consciousness.

At that moment, the pressure on his neck eases and the creature's claws release. He feels the air rush into his lungs and his strength returns. He pushes the creature away, which stumbles back a few steps. He runs after it and pushes the creature with all his might into a mirror. It falls with a crash against the mirror, which shatters with a loud crack. The creature falls through it, plunging into an abyss behind it.

The broken mirror reveals the view outside. He sees the Ferris wheel, glowing as it spins in circles. Abelia is still sitting alone in the gondola, her gaze sadly fixed on the night sky. Then the Ferris wheel suddenly starts to sway. The earth begins to shake, causing the wheel to tilt more and more from side to side. Finally, the wheel passes the centre of gravity and it tilts.exactly in the direction of the maze. First in slow motion, then faster and faster, it moves inexorably towards the maze, accompanied by a deafening crunching sound.

At that moment, Jack opens his eyes, startled. He rubs his sleepy eyes and sighs with relief. Abelia is no longer sitting opposite him. She is sitting beside him again. She has leaned her head against his shoulder and is sleeping peacefully. Her nostrils move gently as she breathes. Her lips are closed except for a small gap through which her teeth gleam.

Jack smiles at the sight of her eyes, her lips and the soft skin, which he caresses with his gaze. He tries to interpret her expression, but fails. She doesn't look worried, but she doesn't look carefree either, neither happy nor sad, neither angry nor peaceful. She just leans her head against his shoulder and sleeps peacefully.

Jack would like to take her in his arms, but doesn't for fear of waking her. Her head triggers a gentle pressure on his shoulder. Her hair smells of apple, which reminds Jack of their first encounter. He breathes in the scent deeply and leans his head against hers.

Inspector Hartmann and his colleague Hempel walk past the compartment, seemingly uninterested. But then they turn around, stop in front of the door and stare at Jack. They stand motionless for a few moments, then open the door but don't enter, instead standing on the threshold.

"As promised, we haven't forgotten you," says Inspector Hartmann, whereupon Hempel puts his finger to his lips. "Not so loud, we don't want to wake the lady."

They look at Abelia with mocking grins. They scrutinise her from head to toe, casting long glances at her breasts and between her slightly open, loosely stretched legs. Still grinning, Hartmann nudges his colleague and they turn back to Jack.

"Do you remember where you were the hour before the stop?" asks Hartmann in a hushed voice.

"No," Jack replies, trying to appear calm.

"Well then, we'll see if you remember anything in the end," Hartmann says, to which Hempel adds: "We're watching you."

Their faces stiffen as if rehearsed. They stand there for a few seconds and look down at Jack with contempt, then they inspect the room with their eyes as if they can detect something suspicious and close the door without a greeting.

They suddenly stop in the corridor, recoiling in confusion as a tall figure approaches. An old man appears, his hair frizzy and white, with angular features and light blue eyes that give his gaze a penetrating expression. He approaches the compartment without haste, glancing inside in a friendly manner and nodding to himself as if he has found what he is looking for.

He opens the door and smiles warmly at Jack. "Do you have a seat left here?"

"Yes, of course, it's all free," Jack says, making an inviting gesture towards the empty seats.

The old man turns to Hartmann and Hempel and looks down at them sternly. The officers move further back so that Jack can no longer see them, then he hears their footsteps in the distance.

16

The old man comes in slowly and sits down in the middle seat opposite. He carries only a small brown leather travelling bag, which he places on the seat next to him. He is wearing a dark pinstripe suit that looks rather worn. The suit is creased in several places and there are a few stains on the trousers. A dark blue tie, elegantly tied in a large knot, stands out brilliantly. There are no creases or other signs of wear, and the bright blue colour seems to shine. The same goes for the black shoes, the leather of which is immaculate.

"If I may introduce myself, my name is Friedrich van Roit. But I'll be happy if you just call me Friedrich," the old man says with a real glow in his smile.

Jack introduces himself and Abelia, who is still asleep, quietly so as not to wake her.

Van Roit nods attentively, then says: "Pretty curious, those two policemen."

"They've been so persistent all the time. I'm afraid I won't be able to get rid of them any time soon."

"Why do you think you can't get rid of them?"

"I've got myself into some contradictions and I have no idea how to get out of them."

"But Jack, life is full of contradictions. You don't have to worry about that."

"Maybe you're right, but this time it really is a problem."

"Maybe, but let me tell you something, Jack. People spend most of their time worrying about problems that don't exist."

"What do you mean by that? Are you saying the police don't exist?"

"Yes, they do exist. But they will disappear from your life faster than you can imagine."

"I'm afraid it won't be that easy in this case."

"Yes, it is. Give it time, Jack. Many things work themselves out."

Jack smiles as if van Roit's words have lifted a weight from his shoulders. This kind man, turning to Jack in such a friendly manner, seems so familiar to him, as if he has known him for a long time. Perhaps it is the kindness, the charisma, or what he sees of himself in the distant future.

But what is certain is that he believes him, and that gives Jack a feeling of comfort.

"Your girlfriend Abelia is obviously a very heavy sleeper," van Roit says, smiling gently at the sleeping Abelia.

"Yes, she hasn't slept properly for a long time."

"The journey must have been very exhausting for her."

"We've been through a lot together," Jack agrees. "I'm very grateful to have her by my side."

"Grateful is good. But what I find more interesting is, do you feel happy, Jack?"

"Yes, of course," he replies hastily, irritated by the question. He avoids van Roit's gaze, searching for more words to back up his answer, but he can't think of any.

The train passes a pine forest. Mystical and dark, the pine trees stand in rows like a troop of soldiers. The ground is littered with dry pine needles, spread out like a spiky carpet.

In his mind, Jack lights a match and throws it into the forest, where the burning match falls into the spiky carpet and the small flame flares up like an explosion. Then the fire spreads, inexorably taking everything with it until the whole pine forest is ablaze.

"Forgive my indiscretion, Jack. The question was inappropriate." Van Roit pauses for a moment, seemingly pondering the words that follow. "I'm just curious, and if it makes you feel any better, most people are overwhelmed by the question of happiness. In fact, it's not even possible to give a clear answer."

"I'm afraid you'll have to explain that to me."

"Very few people are happy, or at least they don't feel happy."

"Why aren't we happy?" asks Abelia, suddenly wide awake.

Van Roit turns to her as naturally as if she had been part of the conversation the whole time.

"Because people suffer. All people suffer." He speaks the words strongly and clearly, as if worried that something might not be understood.

"And why do we suffer?" Abelia asks impartially, like a curious child.

"People are in a terrible hurry. They are either running from the past or chasing the future. They try to be faster and faster without realising that there is no speed that could make them faster."

"So we would be happier if we slow down?" asks Abelia.

"That would be a start. It's better to just stop and pause for a moment. Just trying to live in the here and now for a while opens up a whole new perspective on life for some people. It doesn't guarantee happiness, but it helps to recognise it."

"Do you always live in the here and now?" asks Jack.

"No, of course not. I always just take my moments, that's enough for me."

"Are you happy?" asks Jack, not afraid to provoke him.

He smiles at him patiently and benevolently. "Sometimes I am, and sometimes I'm not. But it doesn't matter to me, because there can't be happiness all the time. Imagine you were never unhappy. At some point you would no longer know what happiness feels like and how precious it is. It would dissolve all by itself."

"So it needs unhappiness to recognise happiness," Abelia concludes.

"Exactly, my dear. Just as the day needs the night and the night needs the day." Van Roit pauses and smiles. "Or as you both need each other."

The train loses speed and slowly rolls into the next station. Rumbling footsteps can be heard from the corridor. Inspectors Hartmann and Hempel hurry past, take a quick look inside the compartment and hurry on.

Van Roit looks after the officers and takes his bag on his lap with a cheerful smile.

"Well, it's time for me to move on."

He stands and runs his hands over his suit, trying to smooth out the creases, but he doesn't really succeed.

"The conversation with you both was very inspiring. Thank you for the pleasant company and the refreshing conversation. I wish you both all the best," he says, indicating a bow.

"It's been a pleasure, too," Jack says.

As if he hadn't heard the words, van Roit grabs his travelling bag and leaves.

17

The train arrives at the station. A long queue of travellers jostles in the corridor. Some are jostling impatiently, others are stressed by the impatience ones. The clash of extremes creates an invisible tension that turns into a dormant aggression waiting to explode. The tailgaters go a little further than the respectful distance that people keep from each other and almost inadvertently bump into the people in front. The people in front, on the other hand, hesitate a little more, in order to provoke a collision that they can be outraged about.

As the queue finally disperses, the officers reappear, take another quick look at the compartment and start to move on when they suddenly freeze. They stand and stare at the seat where van Roit was sitting a few moments ago.

They open the compartment door and Inspector Hartmann asks: "Where did he go?"

After a moment's hesitation, Jack asks with an indifferent expression: "Who?"

"The old man," says the inspector angrily.

Jack shrugs his shoulders. "No idea."

"You'll know if the man has left or not."

"If he's not here, he's obviously gone," he says with a casual grin.

Hartmann rears up in front of him, Hempel standing beside him, legs apart. "Dude, you want to be cheeky?"

Jack looks at his fingernails. "That's up to you."

"Just be careful, dude. After all, we've still got a score to settle," roars the now flushed Inspector Hartmann, who can no longer hide his anger.

"Oh, you know, Hartmann, you can actually go fuck yourselves, both of you." As soon as he has spoken these words, he is surprised by his own tone of voice. Cheeky and free of any fear or escalation, he hurls the words at the two, who now seem to recoil in bewilderment. The force of the words has not escaped Abelia's attention. Surprised, she looks up at him, a gentle smile flitting across her face.

Hartmann stands there as if petrified, his breathing fast and shallow, his face glowing. Then he takes a big step towards Jack and bends down threateningly. Jack stands up and they stand so close to each other that Jack can smell the odour of sweat and aftershave. Hempel stands next to Hartmann as if ready to pounce. The inspector clenches his fists and says with a snort: "Repeat that, dude."

"Oh, let me tell you something, Hartmann. Just piss off," he throws at him with a contemptuous gesture. A gesture with which he wipes away the officers like old cherry pits that have been scattered haphazardly on the floor.

"That was insulting an officer ... now it's your turn ... and you're a witness," he gasps, pointing at Abelia, who shrugs and says, "I didn't hear anything."

The officers look at each other in disbelief. Their eyes switch between each other and Jack several times. Then Hartmann raises his fist and takes a deep breath as Hempel nudges him from the side, pointing to the platform.

Outside, van Roit is standing on the platform watching the action. Amused, he looks into the compartment and laughs. It is a mocking laugh that shows his teeth. With his sparkling eyes, he cast a spell over the officers, who stare out at him as if hypnotised.

Now he turns his attention to Jack and Abelia. The mocking laughter turns into a warm smile. A silent, mysterious smile that only the three of them understand. A community that will remain an inexplicable mystery to the officers.

Van Roit raises his arm in a final farewell wave to Jack and Abelia. Then his eyes drift back to the officers and he lets out another mocking laugh. He turns around and walks quickly to a staircase.

The officers stand frozen for a moment, as if in a vacuum. Then they rush out of the compartment as if struck by lightning. With a great leap, they jump onto the platform, where they fall down lengthwise from sheer energy. Like in a slapstick scene, they lie on top of each other. Cursing, they get up and stumble towards the stairs. As they turn, they almost fall again, but just manage to keep their balance. Then, like van Roit, they disappear into the darkness.

The officers don't come back and the train continues its journey without them. Jack thinks back to van Roit's words and realises with satisfaction that he was right. Sometimes things take care of themselves. The train picks up speed at a leisurely pace, in no hurry, as if it had all the time in the world, safe in the knowledge that it will arrive anyway.

Abelia looks for Jack's hand and puts hers in it. She strokes the back of his hand with her thumb. The skin on his hand is rough. It's a soft roughness, like fine-grained sandpaper that feels like short-haired fur.

"You've changed," she says in a soft voice.

"For better or worse?"

"Neither, just different."

She takes a smartphone and AirPods out of her bag, puts the AirPods in her ears and scrolls through her playlist for a while. She clicks on a song, thinks for a moment and continues searching. After a while she decides, leans on Jack's shoulder and shortly afterwards the sound of violins can be heard.

Vivaldi's Autumn from the Four Seasons hums from the AirPods. The storm of summer has subsided and the peaceful autumn sounds in a rhythmically lively melody that seems to unite happiness and peace.

Then follows the second part of Autumn, with gentle, peaceful string sounds whose melody covers them like a gentle veil.

The third part comes with powerful rhythms over which a feeling of departure unfolds. The melody sounds so powerful that, despite its festive beauty, it also has something binding and perhaps definitive about it. The sounds flow through the bloodstream to the heart, which catapults the music into the body with powerful beats.

Outside it starts to rain. Small rivulets run down the window pane. Drops form and stick to the glass until they give in to gravity. They run down the window pane, hitting smaller drops and taking those with them. Some drops join together, others separate from each other.

Although the drops behave differently, one thing is always the same. Sooner or later they all start moving, following the course that nature has set for them, inexorably following the laws of nature. The dust on the windscreen is slowly but surely washed away by the rain and the view becomes clearer and clearer.

They sit closely together, feeling each other's warmth, feeling each other's breath, and also that which cannot be perceived with the senses. It is the feeling that cannot be grasped, that cannot be captured or held on to. A feeling that is reserved for only a few people and that always requires someone else to bring the same feeling with them so that they can unite.

They perceive their bodies and feel their hearts taking on the pulsating rhythm of the other as they look out into the rain, nestled together in harmony.

18

The rain lets up and the first rays of the morning sun break through the clouds. The sun is still low and its rays shine into the compartment like a bright spot of light. Jack squints his eyes, Abelia holds a hand protectively over her face. They sit up and stretch, as if they had just woken up from a long sleep.

A young couple in their mid-twenties are standing in the corridor. They stand close together and looking out into the illuminated landscape. When the woman turns around, it is to recognise that she is pregnant. Her belly bulges through her striped dress, which the young woman caresses gently with one hand. The man holds her hips and gently leads her onwards.

Jack is overcome by a melancholy mood, a feeling of finality. He senses that his journey is coming to an end. An end that he has never thought about, but which is now inevitably approaching. It is the knowledge of what is to come, but which he has never thought about. A thousand things run through his mind that still need to be done, but for which there is no more time. For a moment he regrets how much time he has spent on useless things that have taken up so much space that there is no time left for the important things.

But he is also filled with a sense of gratitude. Grateful to have Abelia with him, to feel her warmth and to know that he could always rely on her blindly. She gave him so much without asking for anything in return. She was his partner from the very beginning, never leaving him in any doubt that he could trust her as much as she could trust him. It is a bond that cannot be taken for granted, and he is all the more grateful to have been given this gift.

"Abelia," he says, but she doesn't react. "My last stop is almost here."

A few moments pass. There are moments of silence before Abelia finally replies.

"I know, I've known all along."

He wants to say something else, but he can't find the appropriate words. He wants to explain something for which he himself has no explanation. All he knows is that his journey ends here, whether he likes it or not.

"You don't have to say anything," she whispers, "I understand and I know."

The train slows down. They approach the station inexorably. The houses they are passing become more and more visible, and the clearer they are, the more he realises the finiteness of this journey and the inevitability of its end.

Around them it gets restless, as it always does when they enter a railway station. But this time there aren't many people getting off. Most of them have very little luggage. An older man is carrying a small suitcase, a woman just a handbag. Then a group of backpackers passes by with heavy steps. The backpacks on their backs are so big that they tower over their bodies. As the train pulls into the station, Jack wishes for a moment that the train would just go through. The slower the train gets, the more he wants to hold on until it finally stops and he knows it's time to leave.

Jack stands up, taking his leather suitcase with its now rusty metal fittings from the luggage rack and placing it beside him.

He turns to Abelia, who looks at him with a blank expression. He tries to make out whether she is sad, angry or even happy, but he recognises nothing, nothing at all. There is only a deep emptiness in her gaze, in which nothing can be read.

He takes her hand and their fingertips touch, moving up until their hands clasp one last time. Then she stands up and clings to him tightly. They embrace and hold each other, so close they can hear her pulse beating loudly.

"It's time," he whispers in her ear and gently releases his embrace. She nods, letting go of his embrace and turning away. He picks up his suitcase and turns back to her, but she has turned away. He can't see the tear running down her face.

The pain of parting burns in his chest and he senses that Abelia feels the same. A moment they both knew about, but had never been aware of. Now the moment is here, it has arrived with brutal certainty and leaves no choice. It is difficult for him to take his eyes off her. Finally he overcomes himself and turns, walks out of the corridor and makes his way off the train.

He looks for her compartment on the platform. When he finds it, she is still standing there looking out. He stands in front of the compartment and looks up at her, but she doesn't notice him. She looks past him. He takes a step and stands directly in her line of sight, but she doesn't see him. She looks through him as if he weren't there.

The train starts to move and Abelia is still standing there, looking out aimlessly. He tries to hold her in his gaze for as long as he can. But she disappears from his field of vision, and all he can see is the window, which gets farther and farther away until it is completely blurred. Then he looks at the train, which gets smaller and smaller until it disappears, leaving only the empty tracks.

The platform is visibly emptying. People are walking purposefully, without looking around or to the right or left. They take no notice of anything except what is directly in front of them, and they follow it as if automatically.

Jack looks around and can't see anyone except for an old woman waiting on a wooden bench. The platform is now empty and quiet. A few pigeons are cooing, discarded paper is carried across the platform by the wind, fluttering around uncoordinatedly and making rustling noises.

Now he descends a flight of stairs into a grey tunnel with cold light. It is deserted. Cold tiles, some sprayed with graffiti, line the walls. It is quiet, only his footsteps can be heard, echoing in the cold grey.

He sees himself and Abelia as they first met. How she sat opposite him and reading, while he watched her with fascination. Then he thinks of their first conversations, of getting closer and finally the dance. Time passes before him like a film, as if he were watching a performance by two strangers. He thinks of van Roit's words and wonders what would have been different if he had met him earlier.

He steps out of the station and approaches a park. The sun has risen, the sky is bright blue. A meadow is freshly mown and smells of damp grass.

He has a ghostly image of Abelia in front of him. He tries to remember the details, her eyes, her mouth, her contours... he remembers everything. He has her image before him, as clear as if she were standing in front of him.

He sees her laughing, talking and lying carefree in his arms. He can also feel how it feels when she sighs and cuddles up to him. It's all there and he feels that it's here to stay.

A long tree-lined alley stretches out before him, the leaves of the trees golden yellow, their colours intensified by the sun. He makes his way without haste, accompanied by a shadow that follows him until it gets dark.